The Darkness gathers.
Far away, a woman waits.
Dragons sing danger!

THE LAND OF
TEN THOUSAND WILLOWS

A Fantasy of a China That Never Was

BOOK I:

The Phoenix Bells

BY

Kathryn Grant

ACE FANTASY BOOKS
NEW YORK

For

Bob Vardeman,
a good friend through troubled times,
and always a welcome visitor
in the Land of Ten Thousand Willows

This book is an Ace
Fantasy original edition, and
has never been previously
published.

THE PHOENIX BELLS

An Ace Fantasy Book/published by arrangement with
the author

PRINTING HISTORY
Ace Fantasy edition / March 1987

Cover art by Richard Bober.
Map by Andrea Minasian.

ISBN: 0-441-66227-7

Ace Fantasy Books are published by The Berkley Publishing Group,
200 Madison Avenue, New York, New York 10016.

PRINTED IN THE UNITED STATES OF AMERICA

May the gates of Heaven be opened wide!
In ecstasy I ride the black cloud.
I command the whirlwind to be my herald,
I summon the rainstorm to lay the dust!

Amid the alternations of dark and brightness,
There are none who have known the extent of my power.

I ride the roaring chariots of dragons,
Soaring high into the serene heavens.

The Negative in the place of the Positive—
This is the time of great evil.
Embracing loyalty, but forlorn,
I commence my journeys.

—from poems by Chu Yuan (332–296 B.C.)

Author's Note

While the Land of Ten Thousand Willows is solely the creation of the author (with a very decided influence from pre–Manchu China), several of the places and characters within the book are indeed historical figures from the years 1632-1634, notably the royal figures in Muscovy, France and England, as well as Oliver Cromwell.

Sun, as in the name Ty-Sun, is pronounced "Soon."

A *li* measures approximately one-third of a mile.

COLD MOUNTAINS
COLD MOUNTAIN MONASTERY
LOTUS R
RIVER OF NINE
BAMBOO MARSH
WEST GATE
CAVE OF STONE RAIN
WEST MOUNTAINS
SKY MAIDEN LAKE
THE LAND OF TEN THOUSAND WILLOWS

THE WALL of LIVING STONE
YELLOW POPLAR LAKE
IMPERIAL TOMBS
TOMBS of THE FIRST EMPEROR
IMPERIAL HUNTING FOREST
RIVER of LONGEVITY
EAST GATE
RIVER of PROSPERITY
NINE DRAGON BRIDGE
WILLOW LAKE
DRAGON'S WANDER
WILDERNESS WOODS
LAKE of ASSURED HARMONY
OLD-MAN-GO-BACK MOUNTAINS
©1986

Prologue

Across the world, many thousands of miles distant from the Willow Garden, the One watches, and envies, and hates. There, in the land where it is always spring, the last magical elements of Earth, the dragons, have fled for protection. While they still live, while they flourish, these dragons of old, the Darkness cannot prevail.

And so the Watcher broods, and bides.

PART I

1632

1

In the year known as 1632, it was the first day of the week-long Festival of Lively Intellect in the Land of Ten Thousand Willows.

And Ty-Sun, the One-True and August Emperor and Magician of the Land of Ten Thousand Willows, or Willow Garden as it was also known, Lord of the Sun and the Moon, Son of Heaven, Bearer of the Star Wand, Holder of the Lotus, Guardian of the Dragons of Earth, Protector of Long Life, Wielder of Dragon's Tongue, Warlord of the Wall of Living Stone, Scholar, Poet, Painter, and Dutiful Son of the late Ty-Ch'an, reclined upon a brocade divan made luxurious by dozens of silk pillows, and yawned.

Just five and twenty years of age, Ty-Sun had succeeded to the ancient Dragon Throne upon the death of his father, Ty-Ch'an, only a few months ago. Grief-stricken, he had managed to settle well into his appointed duties in that short time, even though before his father's death he had concerned himself only with the luxuries of the mind and body.

Not only was he the youngest emperor in the Willow Garden's recorded history, but he also stood far taller than any other man, royal or commoner, within the confines of his empire. Like his father and grandfather and great-grandfather before him, he tended toward a certain heaviness, a polite way of saying that he was far from being thin, but yet it was a weight which he carried well upon his large frame.

Men of the Willow Garden were generally heavyset, and Ty-Sun knew he would lose the respect of his subjects if he became as scrawny as the few Westerners admitted thus far to the Garden.

Too, his life was exceedingly good, the days long and languid with little physical activity beyond occasionally strolling through the gardens. There were many hours in which to drink cinnamon wine and to nibble upon sugared plum blossoms, or toasted almonds or coconut monkeys, as the confections were known.

Delicate sheaths of embossed silver protected his long fingernails, and the metallic guards clicked musically whenever he gestured. His square face supported a wide forehead and sturdy nose, and his cheekbones, where they could be detected, slanted high. His almond-shaped eyes were a deep rust-brown flecked with gold, and he wore his shoulder-length black hair straight, restrained only by two small silver pins shaped like phoenixes. He was clean-shaven, for by the Willow Garden's standards he was yet a youth, but he would be expected to cultivate a beard when he was some years older.

His robes were the most magnificent silk spun in the Garden. His tunic of deep gold, cinched at the waist by a wide belt of black silk, ended at the ground with matching fringe. The tunic's sleeves, wide at the shoulder, narrowed somewhat as they reached the wrist, and were so long that they covered almost the entire hand. Over that he wore still another tunic, this one sleeveless, but only knee-length; white, it was hemmed with designs of the phoenix and other incredible legendary birds that had once dwelled in the Garden.

Large round medallions of red and black five-clawed, or *lung*, dragons in glorious designs encircled his bronze-colored outer garment. Stylized flames extensively decorated the dragon robe, too, interspersed with the Twelve Symbols of Authority, which expressed his symbolic rulership of the Universe. On his feet he wore soft black slippers with leather soles, while atop his head he wore a headdress in the shape of a flat board from which hung, front and behind, thirteen pendants of colored pearls on red strings.

On his lap a tiny dog, scarcely larger than a man's hand, lay curled in sleep. Its wide face seemed almost too small for its comically large eyes, and its nose was very short, almost as if it had once walked into a wall. Its fur was a greyish brown, and around its small neck it wore a collar of hammered gold.

Ty-Sun yawned once more and stroked the long silken hair of the dog, which murmured in its sleep. Around him a handful of his numerous concubines ministered to his moment-to-moment needs so that he would have no need to stir himself.

Presently one handed him his fan of gilt paper when a warm breeze wafted across his face, while another fed him water chestnuts and candied almonds and other delights. A third brought a cup of blue enamel, gold wire worked into the shapes of dragons and pheasants on its side, filled with apricot wine and raised it to her lord's lips when he gestured with one long finger. Still a full half-dozen others waited, all of them dressed in their finery and sitting primly on silken pillows until their lord beckoned for them to come forward.

He had already visited with his various governmental ministers that morning, taking care of the little business that was left for the day, and then he had retired to his rooms.

In honor of the festival, the third already proclaimed this month, Ty-Sun had been listening sleepily to the lulling tones of his favorite concubine, Spring Rain, as she read his latest work. It was a poem of love, and having just finished it that morning after rising a full hour earlier than usual so that he could set to work, he had asked her to read it aloud so that he might consider its merit.

There had been no time earlier in the day for her to do so, and now the sun was already beginning to slant through the drooping branches of the willow trees that surrounded the great palace like a green wall, and occasionally the light would flicker across his robes, and the gold threads would shine like stars. Soon, the light would fade, the stars would come out slowly one by one, and it would be evening, and time for his large meal of the day.

Spring Rain's voice stopped when she saw his eyes flicker shut, but he struggled to open them again and indicated she should continue.

"The dying plum blossom falls from the branch, swirling downward into the blue water, and there it drifts away, as your love has fled from me."

He smiled, pleased with an effort that had cost him only a few minutes of his life. Perhaps he would write several others for the festival. The concubines sitting close by him, Gold Lotus, Never Grieve, and Yeh Tsu-ying, clapped with great admiration.

Spring Rain, a tiny woman with waist-length hair that sparkled as though carved of jet, set the scroll down on an octagonal sandalwood table nearby and waited. She did not clap as had the others. Her nose was short, her mouth small, and her eyes as dark as the fruit of the mulberry and as large as a doe's. Her eyebrows arched in a feathery line, the result of many hours' work training them thusly. She wore a tunic of peach silk, its hem sewn with black thread, trousers of white, and black embroidered cloth slippers. Moonstone earrings dangled from her dainty earlobes.

It was often whispered by the concubines, who had little more to do than to gossip about their "sisters," that Spring Rain was of *peasant* origin. Not in the least shamed by this, the girl spoke frequently of life in her home village in the tall and rugged Cold Mountains far to the north. She was only eighteen years old, and had come to the court the previous year after Ty-Sun, then the Royal Prince, had ridden through her village and spotted her as she worked in the fields with her family. He had arranged with her parents for her to come with him, and whenever she wished, she could go visit her parents and sisters—providing she returned to court.

"What did you think?" he asked, his eyes closed now as he recalled the images of the fragile white petals skimming along the water's surface. Blue and white . . . the colors of heaven . . . an excellent image. He valued her opinion, for while she had no formal education before she came to the palace, she understood and loved poetry—unlike the other concubines—and often, late into the night they would read poems together. Several times she had turned her hand to composing poems, and each one, while modest, had been applauded by him.

She hesitated only a little. "I think it was a fair poem, my lord."

A black eyebrow lifted high in surprise. "You say a 'fair' poem?"

Never Grieve clapped a plump hand to her tiny painted mouth and darted horrified glances at Ty-Sun, then at the offender. Gruesome scenes of Spring Rain's impending punishment cartwheeled through her mind as she gripped the shoulder of Yeh Tsu-ying so that she would not collapse in a faint. Gold Lotus made a small mewing sound, almost a moan, as she waited for the emperor's well-known fierce temper to assert itself. Yeh Tsu-ying, only vaguely aware that her shoulder was numb from being pinched, sat frozen, staring at Spring Rain as if the girl had sprouted a second head.

As court favorite, Spring Rain had the right given to few to speak more openly than the others. It was not a right that she often or casually employed, because with her shrewd good sense she knew that when the emperor claimed he wanted candor from her, he really wished unqualified approval.

"Yes, my lord. I do not think it was your best work. You have done better in the past, yet this is not too uneven."

He was astonished by her response and opened his mouth to sternly admonish her, even though he rather suspected she was correct, then decided he would do no such thing. Today, after all, was the Festival of Lively Intellect, and as a citizen of the Willow Garden she had the right to criticize his creative endeavors on this day. No, he would do nothing.

Breaths held, the concubines waited. Spring Rain's hands

were clasped loosely in front of her. If she was nervous, she did not show it.

The handsome emperor smiled benevolently, almost indulgently. Generally his good mood prevailed, and it was only upon rare occasions that his anger rose, although when it did it was as fierce as the breath of Wind Mother. This was not to be such an occasion. He was too comfortable to stir himself.

Spring Rain, more relieved than she looked, bowed in his direction and slowly released the breath she too had held so long.

"More wine, my lord?" she asked.

"Yes."

She filled his cup with cinnamon wine, a treat he dearly loved, then poured herself some and drank it quickly. The coolness of the liquor settled the heat that had been racing through her cheeks. For a moment she had feared she had gone too far with him, but all was fine now. Gracefully she sat upon a large silk pillow next to the couch. He smiled down at her.

He drained his cup and held it out. Gold Lotus rose to pour more wine, while Never Grieve brought him a silver plate heaped with sesame seed balls, which, when one bit into them, oozed a deliciously warm and sweet plum filling.

"Tsu-ying," he said.

The concubine leaped to her feet, and bowed before him. In her hands she held a *qin*, a seven-stringed long zither without frets. She wore a silk robe the color of fresh mint closely buttoned to the neck, with a white satin collar clasped around her throat. The robe covered her feet, so that only the tips showed when she moved. Over this dress, she wore another heavily embroidered robe whose sleeves would have swept the ground if she had not taken care to prevent it. Her face was very white from a special make-up she made herself, while carmine stained her cheeks and lips. Her eyebrows, like those of Gold Lotus and Never Grieve, were only the width of a single hair, and she had painted them green. It was, Ty-Sun recalled, a style in imitation of the kingfisher.

She sat opposite him and plucked the zither's strings, and as the light music rose around him, Ty-Sun closed his eyes once more.

He loved music in its numerous forms, and could easily listen for hours to the *qin*, or the *pipa*, a four-stringed pear-shaped lute. Most of all, though, he loved the high pure sound of the female voice, and often commanded that his concubines sing to him by the hour.

When he heard no more music he realized he had been asleep a few minutes, then roused himself and smiled in Yeh Tsu-ying's direction. Her plump cheeks were streaked with tears at what she had thought was his disapproval. Once he smiled, though, her tears dried up, and she began playing a lively melody that he had written last month for the Dragon Boat Festival.

"Thank you," he said when she was finished. She bowed to him, rose to her feet and backed away until she reached her own pillow once more.

The concubines stared at him, waiting. He ate several more honeyed figs and drank more wine with its wonderful cinnamon aroma, then decided it was time for some stimulating conversation.

He yawned once, then softly clapped his hands together and in a flash of dazzling crimson light three figures appeared before him. All bowed, and Ty-Sun inclined his head slightly toward the two gods and one goddess who had come at his summons. They, and the other inhabitants of Tian, or Heaven, always came at his beckoning so that they could visit or encourage him in the magic ways which they had taught him.

The god standing to one side was the Second Lord, Erh-lang. With him was the Celestial Dog, T'ien-kou, a canine of massive proportions around whose neck was a collar of beaten gold. Erh-lang himself wore robes the color of leaves in the autumn, embroidered with gold cranes. He was a sturdy youth, who looked the same age as the emperor. He was a handsome fellow, too, although he acknowledged that he was not as good-looking as Ty-Sun.

The two other heavenly entities were the Emperor Kuan, Kuan-ti, god of war; and the Princess of Streaked Clouds, Sheng-mu, who protected women and children. Kuan-ti was dressed all in green and had a round face as red as a jujube fruit, while Sheng-mu had the appearance of a beautiful young woman dressed in robes of apricot and pale dawn light. Silver moons and suns decorated her exquisite garment.

"My uncle, the August Personage of Jade, sends you greeting, Lord Ty-Sun, on this most important day of the year," Erh-lang said as he stepped forward.

"And you must convey my best wishes to him," he replied.

He always enjoyed visiting with Erh-lang, and they had spent many long hours talking and playing chess in the past.

Kuan-ti, who wore a fierce expression at all times, beetled his thick eyebrows, and his scowl deepened. "Why have you summoned us, Your Majesty?" he demanded with his usual lack of refined manners. "Is it time for your practice?"

"It is indeed, Lord Kuan-ti. It has been some time since we four met, and I thought today would be appropriate."

"Good." Kuan-ti sighed gustily. "I wish to test you most thoroughly this time. You have much improvement to make."

Erh-lang flashed a look of amusement at Ty-Sun, who smiled in return. He was accustomed to the brusque ways of Kuan-ti, who was almost as abrupt as Ty-Sun's army commander. Almost.

The three gods arranged themselves around the emperor, while he offered them refreshments. Then he raised his long hands. Bright jagged lightning, normally the product of Tien Mu or Mother Lightning, flashed within the palace bower, only inches away from the ceiling.

The abrupt noise deafened the concubines, who slapped their hands over their ears. Only Spring Rain did not flinch; instead she watched avidly as Ty-Sun's hands traced complicated patterns in the air, as though performing a stately dance. Suddenly peach blossoms showered upon the women.

They giggled as they snatched the fragrant flowers out of the air and slid them into their hair. Pleased with this rather easy effort, Ty-Sun nodded to himself. A look of concentration fell over his face as once more he moved his hands, this time the patterns growing fiercer. Tiny fires the color of copper burst into flames along the perimeter of the marble floor.

Gold Lotus and Never Grieve gasped, but before the fires spread, fleecy clouds as small as the flames appeared and rained silver droplets.

"Excellent," murmured Kuan-ti. "Your magic is good as always."

"Thank you, my lord." Kuan-ti had never once criticized him, but he knew the god would not fail to do so when he thought it appropriate.

"And the others?" asked Sheng-mu. "Will you not show us how you progress in other ways?"

"Very well, Your Highness," Ty-Sun murmured. He raised his hands and the nail guards clinked musically. He knit his brow, straining now, for he wished to conjure up a living organism, the great Lion, a mythical creature which was rumored to have dwelled once in the Land of the Ten Thousand Willows.

He sensed a stirring in the air around him, and suddenly the great room darkened. Frightened, Never Grieve gave a piercing cry, then leaped up. Beneath Ty-Sun's feet, the tiled floor began to heave, as if something large had been sleeping in the earth and was just now awakening. The floor shuddered once, then twice, and Never Grieve was tossed off her feet. She fell close to Spring Rain, who helped the weeping woman to the pillows.

Ty-Sun frowned. This wasn't right. The Lion should be forming now, and instead . . . instead he saw . . . only darkness, darkness like splashed ink. It was spreading around him, swallowing and suffocating him as it pressed as close to him as a lover. He knew he must do something. The air was being squeezed from him even as he stood there, and he began coughing. With great difficulty Ty-Sun lifted his arms and moved his lips. Orange lightning flashed, piercing the black shroud, and slowly the darkness, like fog, dissipated.

"That was most spectacular," Sheng-mu murmured. She clapped enthusiastically, as did the other two gods, who were nodding to one another.

The darkness had not been deliberate upon his part, and Ty-Sun wondered what had gone wrong. He had been about to call up the Lion, but something had interfered. He glanced at Spring Rain, and saw that her face mirrored his own concern. Of all those who had witnessed the unusual occurrence, only she suspected that he had had no control over it.

He pushed back his hair which had come loose from its pins, then settled upon his cushions. Gold Lotus poured more wine for him, and gave him more figs and rice balls, but he only nibbled at them. He was still disturbed by the . . . ripple . . . he had felt, the ripple as if something had been reaching out toward him. He shuddered, then returned his attention to his divine guests. He mustn't be rude.

"The festival goes well, my lord Erh-lang. We have been celebrating all of today, and tonight, when darkness falls, we will light the lanterns and have the readings of the poems."

When darkness falls. . . . Once more a shudder passed through Ty-Sun. Tonight, the darkness would not be as friendly as it usually was.

"Have you written a poem for this occasion, Lord Ty-Sun?" Sheng-mu inquired.

"Why yes, my lady. It is a poem of love. Here, I shall read it for you."

He beckoned to Spring Rain, who presented the emperor with the paper. He cleared his throat and began reading his latest creation. His mind was only half on his words, the other half remembering the unexpected darkness that had spread through the room. What had that been? And why had it come to him?

When he finished, the divine personages applauded and complimented him on his poetic effort. In turn they read poetry of their own creation. Later they began chatting of the news in Heaven, while Ty-Sun leaned back to listen. Outside the magnificent palace of marble and ivory, he heard the reassuring call of the dragons as they wandered through the beautiful willows that gave the land its name.

Ty-Sun, like his forebears, had been commanded by the gods to guard the dragons for as long as they dwelled within the confines of the Garden. The dragon's call was called the phoenix bells, and only one destined to walk with the dragon could hear the incredibly high-pitched sound—a sound that only he within the Willow Garden could hear. The dragons made other sounds, too, sounds that court members and such could hear, but these were deeper noises, rumblings that gave the dragons their fierce reputation.

Many centuries before, the first dragon had come to the Garden, having fled the west and the errant knight of Europe who sought only to destroy the beautiful creatures. Thereafter, more dragons came, until one day not a single dragon remained outside the Garden. All dwelled happily within, guarded by Ty-Sun's ancestors.

He smiled as he thought of the beautiful and terrible wards. Tonight he would go to them. Tonight.

As he glanced at a black marble and jade fountain carved in the shape of nightingales, then listened to the gold windchimes that whispered softly, he thought it was hard to imagine anything as terrible as that darkness had been. He breathed deeply of the air, redolent of cinnamon and other spices that were burned as incenses, and he knew that he would restore his peace of mind only in the presence of the dragons.

He smiled in anticipation.

2

Moonlight touched Ty-Sun's face, and he awoke instantly. Confused momentarily, he glanced around his bedchamber, then remembered that tonight he was alone. So much the better, he thought as he rose quietly and found his robes folded carefully across a low chair alongside the bed. Light poured through the window covered with silk-gauze screens as he slipped into his robes, paused at the foot of his bed to pet the dog, who'd awakened, then stepped to the door of the room.

He heard no one beyond the door. Doubtless even the handful of guards always stationed outside his rooms were asleep after many long hours of celebrating the first night of the festival, a night of phoenix-pipes and dragon-flutes. He had been alone by his own choice. Gold Lotus had begged to stay, while Never Grieve had wept when he said he wished to sleep by himself tonight. Only Spring Rain had said nothing. He had known she would understand.

He slipped past the bamboo screen that was rolled down each night over the open door to keep errant nightdrafts away from the imperial neck and head. On the Porch of Red Snow he shivered because the night air was cooler than he'd anticipated, and for a moment he wished he had tossed a cloak across his shoulders.

The perfume of autumn orchids and chrysanthemums scented the air with their spicy fragrances, while moonlight painted the Imperial Palace buildings silver. The light glinted off the gently uptilted tiled roofs, blurring the yellow and red and blue, turning them all a faint grey. Crickets chirped from their hiding spots in the gardens, while dragonflies flitted through the air, and off to his left a gentle breeze stirred the long graceful willow branches.

From where he stood he could see beyond to the Imperial City, where at this hour only a few lights dotted the blackness. Scented streets and purple paths. A city sleeping, which was what he should be doing even now. But he couldn't go back to bed, not until he had walked among them one more time.

There were only two ways to leave the huge island on which the Imperial City and Palace sat—if one did not use a boat. The most common way was the Bridge of Ancestors leading from the city across the Willow Lake northward to the farming communities there. The other means belonged only to the Emperor.

He returned to his room, went past the carved mahogany bed built specially to accommodate his long form, then pushed aside a tapestry depicting the rich and varied life of the rogue poet Li Po. Behind was a black lacquered door; he was the only one in the entire palace who possessed a key to its lock.

And behind the door was a tunnel.

He entered the tunnel quickly and quietly, having done this very thing many times in the past. Even when his father had been alive, Ty-Sun had used the tunnel, for these had been the quarters of the royal prince. His father had not known about the secret door and tunnel, and Ty-Sun had only learned of it at the death bed of his father's favorite eunuch, when the wizened old man had beckoned to the prince to come closer and had then passed on his knowledge of it.

The tunnel was not overly long, and fairly dry. It was lined with dark terra-cotta tiles, and it opened on the other side of the city's wall into bushes thick with crimson flowers.

Ty-Sun brushed a fallen petal from his sleeve, and smiled. He was only steps away from Nine Dragon Bridge arching across the Willow Lake.

Not pausing to gaze down into the green depths of the swirling water as he had done on countless other nights, he crossed the marble bridge to the other side, Dragon's Wander, where the dragons of the Land of Ten Thousand Willows roamed free.

Jade mists rose from the dense bamboo groves dotting the island as he walked away from the bridge and passed the ruins of Green Dragon Turret. Ancient almond trees, their grey gnarled branches wrapped in moss like filmy silks, bent this way and that, their features formed long ago by winds. As he stopped at one tree, a flock of bats burst from its uppermost branches. He smiled at the sign of good luck.

The wind, like barely heard voices, whispered to him, while at times an unseen something seemed to pluck at his robes. This was a *shen* place, a place of invisible spirits. He remembered the first time he had come here—something white had glimmered as it paced through the marshes by the bridge, and he had thought he had glimpsed the ghost-tiger. But he had never seen the creature, not in all the years he had been sneaking away from the palace. Perhaps some night he would be lucky enough to meet the ghost-tiger.

He walked down a short avenue, paved with broken stone. On either side loomed statues of great serpents and tigers, camels and lions, all of them fashioned years ago by the first emperor.

Beyond this was marshy land, and he chose his way carefully. A precarious step here or there would land him unexpectedly in the fen, and he didn't want such a cold bath tonight. Wild grass, green and misty, muffled his footsteps.

So far he had heard nothing beyond the usual rustlings of the night, and so he whistled softly.

Doubtless the beasts were curled asleep amidst the bamboo, as was their custom, yet he knew that his whistle would rouse them.

He heard a faint snorting, a deep rumble, then a high-pitched trilling. The phoenix bells. Finally, he heard the sound of something trampling through the reeds and bamboo. After a moment, he saw the movement of the great beasts as they awoke and stretched.

The dragons roared in greeting as he strode toward them. Smoke curled upward from their wide nostrils, and one younger dragon trilled, the sound rippling through the night air.

He stepped among them, running his hands over the dry scales of emerald and crimson and gold along the ridges of their spines, caressing them as though they were his cats or dogs. The smaller ones, their necks reaching only to his waist, rubbed their heads against his legs, reminding him of his faithful little Ch'u.

An older dragon, a veteran of many battles long ago in England, flapped her wings, a fluttering motion that swept a cool breeze across Ty-Sun's face. Her eyes glittered with intelligence.

"Good evening, Madame Shou," he said formally as he bowed.

She nodded her massive head and blew steam toward him. Her name meant longevity, and as close as his father and he could calculate when she first came to live with them, this scarred and somewhat ragged dragon was close to a thousand years old. The others were far younger, some no more than a century old.

Once, there had been many thousands of dragons in the world, but they had been hunted down almost to the point of extinction, and those who had survived the persecutions had fled to the Willow Garden to join their brethren already there. Ty-Sun recalled that as a boy he had witnessed the arrival of dragons from other lands, and he had thrilled at the sight of the skies darkened with the beautiful creatures.

"As long as they stay with us," his father had said, "they will live, and the Earth will live. But if something should happen to them, in this last refuge . . ." Ty-Ch'an had not continued, but the emperor hadn't needed to. With a shudder the young prince had known what his father meant. If something should happen to these dragons, then all life in the Garden, all life—human, animal, plant—on earth, would end.

The dragons shifted aside, letting him step among them. He greeted each by name. He knew them all, as though the beasts were old friends, and as he walked with the dragons, flanking him and following in his footsteps, Ty-Sun felt the uneasiness that had remained with him all day finally begin to recede.

Throughout his life Dragon's Wander had been his sanctuary. Even now.

He had never come here with anyone else, only by himself. Alone always.

He paused to select a few leaves of the herb called dragonleaf. He fed a dragon on his left, who trumpeted its appreciation, then he held out a choice leaf to Madame Shou. The younger dragons pressed eagerly against him, wanting to be hand-fed, too.

Loneliness. That's what it was.

He was lonely, he knew, despite the large number of people whom he saw each day, each night. Hundreds swept through his life daily, servants and soldiers and citizens, concubines and remote relatives, bureaucrats, petitioners come for favors, and despite the constant companionship, he was lonely. Lonely in the midst of the chaos that was court life, lonely in the crowds of hundreds of courtiers and their ladies.

Something was missing from his life.

A faint smile curved his lips. Doubtless his friend General Soong would call that missing substance stimulation, and perhaps the old warrior was correct. But there was something more, Ty-Sun thought, more than intellectual stimulation or whatever Soong would claim.

Perhaps he felt he lacked a purpose in his life. Yet he had but a single obligation that mattered above all else. He must protect the dragons.

And in return, what did he receive? His life, his country,

the loyalty of his people. The knowledge that the Garden, and Earth, were both safe. What more could he want?

He didn't know, but there was something more, he sensed, something lacking in his life, something that he was not receiving. His servants served him out of loyalty, some out of devotion to first his father, then to him. His concubines . . . as for them, he wasn't so sure what motivated them. Certainly they all loved him, he suspected, each in her own way, as father, husband, nephew, however.

Except for Spring Rain, of course. He knew that she loved him, loved him with all her heart, and it saddened him because both knew that she could never be anything more than his favorite concubine.

He cared greatly for her, too, but his heart was not deeply touched.

And perhaps that was what he felt was missing.

Poetry came, unbidden to his mind.

Since you went away, / Gold and green hairpins have lost their glint. / My longing thoughts of you, like sun and moon, / Circling round and round, rise day and night.

He was longing for someone he had never known, would perhaps never know within his life.

Longing . . .

He shrugged. Whatever it was, he would not discover it tonight. He turned back to the dragons and held out his arms to embrace them.

3

Late on the morning of the second day of the Festival of Lively Intellect, Ty-Sun slept soundly on a bamboo chaise, surrounded by some of his numerous pets. Ch'u, the eldest of the small lion dogs, snored fitfully in his sleep, while his grandson, Wu, slumbered on his back, his paws stuck straight up into the air. The third dog, the son of Ch'u, Lu, dozed in a more dignified position, asleep on one of Ty-Sun's long sleeves. All three dogs possessed the same shade of greyish brown silken hair, although Wu's had some red in it. All had small heads, flat noses, and large moist eyes.

The two cats—Hei, pure black and as sleek as an otter, and Bai, possessing fluffy white fur, a gentle disposition, and with one blue and one gold eye—had curled up together atop the emperor's generous stomach. Little Spider, a chubby brown monkey with a tail twice the length of its body lay just below Ty-Sun's neck so that it looked like a fur collar.

Spring Rain paused in the doorway of the Pavillion of Peaceful Repose and smiled at the tranquil scene before her. The cat Hei opened one golden eye, winked, then closed it and promptly went back to sleep. They all looked so comfortable that she didn't want to disturb them, but she had to wake him.

She knew he had not slept much last night because she had heard him leave his rooms not long after the moon had risen. She was aware of a secret exit within his bedchamber, although she didn't know where it was, and she had stayed awake, listening until he had returned, hours later. She didn't know where he'd gone for so long, but she suspected he had been walking among the dragons. She knew he found comfort there, and it saddened her that she could not be of greater help to him. Once she had been tempted to follow him, yet she had not. That was his own private retreat, and she could not violate it.

She shook herself slightly. Enough of this. He had a visitor. She crossed silently to the bamboo lounge and gently touched the emperor's shoulder.

"My lord, awaken, you have a visitor now." She touched his arm again, almost reluctantly, as if she would be breaking a spell.

Little Spider woke first, chittering with irritation. The two cats rose and stretched, then began kneading another spot, not far from the first. Wu awoke with a start and barked in recognition when he saw her. She smiled as she stroked his head and he licked her hand.

"My lord," she said again, this time louder.

One imperial eye opened.

"A visitor has come to see you," she announced. The imperial eyelid began to droop. "My lord," she said, adopting a more severe tone.

He sighed. "Very well." Both eyes opened and he stared down at the assortment of animals strewn across his body. "I am trapped," he admitted.

She laughed, then began lifting the cats off and setting them upon the carpeted floor. Immediately the offended felines began washing themselves. Ch'u jumped off the chaise to join the cats, as did his son, while Wu looked expectantly at Spring Rain. Smiling, she picked up the puppy, then set him beside the others. The monkey screeched, then climbed up one of the pavillion's supports and chattered noisily.

She helped Ty-Sun sit up. He yawned, then brushed back the long hair which had fallen across his shoulders. A slight noise behind made her turn back to the door where she saw that the visitor had not waited as she had instructed him.

Ty-Sun smiled at Fray Esteban Xavier Navarro Villadiego standing only a few feet away and beckoned for him to enter.

"Father, good day to you."

The slender Jesuit priest bowed deeply. "And to you, Your Majesty."

Spring Rain stepped to one side, and although she should have lowered her eyes, she could not. She watched the Jesuit approach.

"Have you come for our daily discussion?"

"Indeed, I have, Your Majesty. I had hoped you would not forget my appointment, what with the excitement and celebration of the festival."

Villadiego was a slender man, with an angular clean-shaven face. He was not particularly handsome yet somehow arresting with his plentiful dark hair and unusual face. He stood not nearly as tall as Ty-Sun, although he was by no means short, and he had white hands that were thin and soft-looking. Ty-sun often thought that the hands would look better on a eunuch. The priest had a pleasant voice and black eyes that Spring Rain had once compared—unfavorably—to raisins.

Ty-Sun found the priest's age difficult to pinpoint. He could have been anywhere from his late twenties to late forties. Whatever his age, the priest was always energetic, rising well before sunrise each morning to plunge enthusiastically into his daily devotions. He was always ready to debate theology or philosophy with Ty-Sun, or eager to travel about the Garden. He was dressed in the customary black robes of a priest of the Society of Jesus, and he wore a large silver crucifix, secured by a leather thong, around his neck.

Ty-Sun smiled politely. Actually, he had hoped that Fray Villadiego would forget the standing appointment. He had stayed on Dragon's Wander far too long last night, and when he had returned finally to his rooms, he had still not fallen to sleep immediately. Thus, he was extremely tired today when he'd finally awakened, and would have enjoyed slumbering most of the hours away. Now, he would not have that chance.

Yet, he would never turn the priest away from his presence. Although he found the priest's monotheism odd, he was fascinated by the man and by this strange religion he preached.

Just a little over two months ago Fray Villadiego had come to the Willow Garden to set up a church. In Ty-Sun's father's time, there had been another Jesuit, an old man who had died not long after arriving in the Willow Garden. For years, the small Catholic mission that the old priest had managed to establish before he died had remained empty, finally decaying until it was no more than a ruin. It was not long after the death of Emperor Ty-Ch'an that the new priest arrived in the Garden.

The second part of his religious plan, or so Fray Villadiego had announced openly to Ty-Sun upon his first visit to the court, was to convert the Garden's residents to Roman Catholicism. Ty-Sun had not responded to this rather bold statement beyond saying that all religions were welcome in his land, but secretly he had known the mass conversion that Fray Villadiego envisioned would not materialize.

And thus far Ty-Sun had been proved correct. None of the Garden's residents had converted. Not many were willing to turn from the comfortable religion of their ancestors to heartily embrace a relatively recent faith where sacrifice of body and mind was a chief attribute.

Roman Catholicism was far too uncomfortable a religion for Ty-Sun's good subjects, what with its pure offering of self, emphasis on saintliness, its numerous large and little sins, and not least of all, its mortification of the flesh, a notion Ty-Sun thought feebleminded at best. Why would anyone wish to deny himself the comforts and pleasures of life in order to insure a very improbable place in a heaven which sounded very boring?

Fray Villadiego thought Ty-Sun's religion of the *yin* and the *yang*, the two forces which pervaded everything, silly. Once Ty-Sun had tried to explain to the priest how the *yin* represented the earth, the female, the dark, while the *yang* was heaven, male, light. Everything else proceeded from these two, both essential to each other. As one increased, the other decreased. The priest had listened politely, then turned the subject to his own bewildering religion.

But he would listen politely and continue tolerating the Jesuit because he was sincere in his claim that all religions were welcome. He wished to show that he respected other religions —even if he thought them deficient in deities and prolific in hardships—and too, he enjoyed talking with the priest, an individual commanding an extraordinary education.

In fact, it had been Fray Villadiego who had organized only three weeks ago a trip by the Court to the tomb of the First Emperor of the Willow Garden, and there, for the first time, Ty-Sun had studied the excavations which had recently uncovered legions of terra-cotta soldiers and horses, all incredible relics of the reign of his great ancestor. Too, Fray Villadiego was extremely knowledgeable in mathematics, astronomy, and cartography, and already Ty-Sun had benefited by his discussions on these subjects.

Ty-Sun had only the sketchiest details of Villadiego's background. The priest had been born in Madrid, Spain, and his parents had died in the plague of 1599–1600; now he was the only surviving member of the aristocratic Villadiego family.

He was a most interesting, if enigmatic, man, Ty-Sun decided, then shrugged to himself. He would talk with the priest, after all. Perhaps he would learn something of interest.

"Wine, Fray?" he offered.

"Yes, thank you." He sat upon the pillow Ty-Sun indicated, while Spring Rain crossed to a low table that contained goblets and a container of wine. She poured the drink, then handed them to the men. Villadiego accepted his without acknowledgment, while Ty-Sun smiled at her. She stepped back, waiting.

"And what shall we discuss today?" He took a sip of wine.

Ah, it was his favorite. Cinnamon wine. He lifted the goblet to his lips a second time.

"Your Majesty, there are as many subjects to discuss as there are stars in the sky. On which topic does your mind rest today?"

The priest was slippery, he thought. He rarely directly answered a question, somehow always turning it back upon the asker. A clever man.

"We have discussed the stars in the past, Fray, and the making of the weather. There was also the system of the Arabic zero, but I wish to talk with you in depth about that at a later time. Hmm, let me see." He glanced across to Spring Rain and saw the disapproval there. He knew she disliked the priest, but he could not understand why. Fray Villadiego had always been polite to her. "What about religion?"

"A noble subject, Your Majesty."

"And one that could keep us talking for weeks, is that not so?" Villadiego inclined his head slightly. Ty-Sun realized that he had not yet seen the priest take a drink of wine. "Your religion or mine?"

"Perhaps that of another, Your Majesty."

"Oh?" He was finished with his wine already and he signaled to Spring Rain for more. Too, he thought he saw some sugared almonds over there. As if she had read his mind, she returned with his goblet filled and with a blue and white porcelain tray heaped with the sweet nuts. He smiled again.

"Yes."

"The religion, where is it, Fray? My country, yours, or somewhere else in the world?"

"It lies within the boundaries of your own land, Your Majesty."

"A third religion?" Ty-Sun was intrigued, and his voice was filled with an eager marvel that grew as he contemplated this rather novel concept. "This has never happened before, you know. I wonder what brought about its start."

"It would be hard to say, Your Majesty, but it is one which I think you should examine closely before it grows too strong."

"Indeed? What is the name of the faith, if it has one?"

"I believe that it is called shamanism."

Ty-Sun paused with an almond halfway to his mouth. "Shamanism? I don't believe that I am familiar with that sect."

"More of a cult, Your Majesty. I understand the leader of this so-called religion calls himself a priest, and he dresses in the hides of animals. They worship animals." The priest's voice held contempt.

"What animals?"

"I beg your pardon?"

"What animals do they worship?"

"Various beasts, which they include in their primitive rites," the priest replied somewhat vaguely, then his voice grew stronger. "As well as members of the cat family. The lion and the tiger." Villadiego's head jerked around as Hei jumped onto the lounge alongside Ty-Sun and stared, unblinking, at the priest.

Ty-Sun saw Spring Rain hide a smile, and quickly had to keep from smiling himself. From the priest's uneasy expression, Ty-Sun judged he must be nervous around cats. Ty-Sun had heard of such fears, but had never given them a second thought. How could anyone fear a cat, or a dog? They were hardly ferocious beasts.

"Come now, I can see no harm in worshipping a cat or a catlike creature, Fray Villadiego. Did not the ancient Egyptians have Bast, the magnificent cat goddess? There was also, I believe, Tefnut, the lion goddess. The cat is honored, as well as being the symbol of good luck in my country."

"So that is true, Your Majesty—in your land. However . . ." And here the priest leaned forward. Hei had settled into a crouch beside the emperor and still stared at the Spaniard, her yellow eyes seeming to burn into him. He would not look at her. "However," he repeated, "in numerous other lands, the cat is regarded as an evil creature. Often it is the familiar of witches and sorcerers, and other perverted practitioners of the black arts."

"So you have said."

"Also, the cat is a carrion creature."

"The cat," Ty-Sun said as he stroked the black cat alongside him, "is a great hunter—or huntress, as is my little gem here." She purred loudly, rubbing her head against his hand, but her eyes stayed on the priest. "She is a delight to watch in her strategy, and I think that soldiers could learn from her."

"She cruelly plays with and tortures the innocent creatures she catches."

"She eats that which she catches, unlike man who tortures simply for pleasure or for gain of worldly goods." Ty-Sun's smile was quickly fading. "That is something which I understand your Inquisition participates in all too frequently."

"It is not my Inquisition, Your Majesty," the priest said stiffly.

"It is an institution of your church," said Ty-Sun easily, "and thus by extension is it not a part of your religious tenets?"

Spring Rain did not wait to hear the priest's answer, but instead slipped outside to return to the main palace to have Never Grieve replace her in the care of her lord. Two of the dogs trotted after her.

Since his unfortunate arrival in the Willow Garden and introduction at Court, Fray Villadiego had been highly visible, and Spring Rain had made no secret of her dislike of the priest.

Once she overheard him telling her master that concubinage was a great sin, and that Ty-Sun should become a member of his religion and dismiss his concubines. The emperor had merely smiled neutrally. She believed that if Fray Villadiego had his way he would change all that Ty-Sun held dear.

No, she didn't like the man, and further, she distrusted him. She had no reason to, yet there was something about him . . . perhaps the way she caught him looking at her at times. It was not the look of a man for a woman. Or perhaps it disturbed her, this way in which he stared at the cats, the other concubines, even at Ty-Sun upon occasion.

Spring Rain didn't understand what it was that marked the Jesuit priest, only that she knew she must be vigilant at all times. For her sake, and for Ty-Sun's. Perhaps she should burn some incense sticks to Sheng-mu. It could not hurt.

4

When Fray Villadiego left some time later to return to his church, Ty-Sun stretched and rose, then left the pavillion. Outside, willow branches trailed through the reflecting ponds built around them, and he breathed deeply of the fresh air. To his left stretched a bed of irises, purple and gold and copper in the afternoon light. Farther down the lane set a garden of white flowers. The Garden of Clouds, he called it, and he liked to stroll through it when he was depressed.

Now, he supposed he shouldn't. He should return to the Inner Court, and yet he was reluctant. He wanted to stay outside for a little longer. Behind him Never Grieve and several servants waited patiently for him to make up his mind. He waved to them, indicating that they should go on without him.

He set off in a northerly way, down a straight walk that would eventually take him to General Soong's outpost. Here were the barracks and stables, and the Tower of Tranquil Gardens, one of the four palace towers. Opposite it was the Tower of Auspicious Clouds, adjacent to the palace kitchens, while closer to his private quarters were the Tower of Raining Flowers and the Tower of Beautiful Views.

He paused, considering, then: let them wait, he decided. He walked along the twisting path of red and white marble and entered the Tower of Beautiful Views through the lacquered door. Slowly, holding up his dragon robe so that the hem would not catch, he climbed the numerous steps to the top of the tower and stared at the vista presented to him. In the distance south of Willow Lake lay the dark and mysterious Wilderness Wood where his father had taken him once to hunt. Farther south he saw the purple haze of Old-Man-Go-Back mountains, where, legend said, orchids of silver and gold covered the rocky sides, in profusion.

Opposite was Dragon's Wander, shrouded in mists day and night, and a patchwork of rich fields surrounding the lake like a comforting blanket.

The air in the tower was cool, a brisk breeze blowing, and far above he watched the swooping flight of falcons and crows.

Tomorrow was the Seventh Moon, the festival of the Hungry Ghosts. On that day the citizens of the Imperial City prepared food for the ghosts with no descendants to care for them, and thus always hungry. Lotus-flower lamps would be carried by men and women through the streets of the city, or else at dusk candles would be stuck into tiny boats and floated across the Lake. And the moon after that was the Eighth, time of harvest. Moon after moon followed, the rituals always the same.

Once more a feeling of sadness enveloped him, and he turned away.

Perhaps later he would go riding. It had been a long time since he had been on a horse. He closed his eyes, and remembered how it had been when he had been the Prince. Daily he had ridden out from the Imperial City to explore the Cold Mountains far to the north and the Lotus River, its source high in that range. He had visited with the monks of Cold Mountain Monastery, then had turned his horse eastward to follow the River; he had fished in the Yellow Poplar Lake, then had gone farther east, then south to follow the course of the River of Prosperity. He had spent the night in the Wilderness Wood, and along the banks of the River of Nines, far to the west. He had travelled several times to the West Mountains, and had seen the Cave of Stone Rain, although he had not gone inside it. He had ridden through every *li* of the Garden, had stopped and chatted with the villagers, with farmers ankle-deep in their rice fields, with merchants he met along the imperial roads.

All of that had happened so long ago. Now, he travelled no longer. There was never time, never opportunity.

Crimson reins, scarlet bridle, crop of coral, jade saddle, embroidered blanket, bit of gold. . . . Like the old poem, he thought with a sad smile.

What had happened to his old pony? He would ask Soong. And perhaps today or tomorrow he would have the pony saddled and go riding.

But now, he knew he must return; he had lingered long enough. Sighing deeply, he left the Tower and its path, and passed ranks of azaleas and peonies, pink cardamom and a reflecting pond. The cats followed him discreetly, although Hei stopped momentarily at water's edge to gaze down at a flash of gold.

He went up gold-inlaid steps and settled in the Hall of Food to dine upon an early afternoon meal of spiced peaches, fish broiled with peppers, and white rice with raisins and almonds.

It was not a lengthy repast, and shortly after he returned to his small audience chamber where he would sit for the remainder of the afternoon to hear the business of the court. Fray Villadiego made an appearance, bowed, and the emperor had no more than leaned back and lifted a hand to indicate he would listen to the first petitioner when he heard a commotion from outside the hall. He glanced at Spring Rain, who sat to his left, then down the length of the low table just as the red lacquer doors burst open.

Striding across the marble floor toward the dais was his most trusted advisor, General Soong Kee Yang.

Soong was also the commander-in-chief of the imperial army, and while formally addressed as "Your Excellency," he preferred the use of his old military title. Short, with sturdy legs, he possessed muscular arms and shoulders and a thick chest with no fat upon it. He spoke bluntly, almost brusquely, at times, and Ty-Sun appreciated that trait in him, even though it was sometimes irritating.

The general wore his white hair long and flowing, had a drooping white moustache, and fierce dark eyes set in a round face, darkened by many decades' exposure to the sun. He never claimed to be a scholar, and the knowledge he owned was all of a practical nature. He wore a two-piece outfit consisting of a long, belted tunic of brown, topped by a jacket, and wore well-crafted black leather boots.

Soong lifted an eyebrow at the sight of the Jesuit priest, and waited while Ty-Sun roused himself.

"General Soong! Well met, old friend! What brings you here . . . so hastily and noisily?"

Soong stroked his moustache and spoke without preamble. "I regret to inform you, Your Majesty, that only a few hours ago my men and I were attacked on the other side of the West Mountains by bandits, who dared scale the Wall of Living Stone."

The Wall of Living Stone protected the Willow Garden from the Outside, and within Ty-Sun's memory, and for that matter anyone else's, no one had scaled the Wall; those permitted to enter traditionally came through either the West Gate or the East. One did not enter by climbing the Wall.

"Impossible!" Ty-Sun smiled somewhat sleepily. Surely this was some jest of the general's. His eyes began drifting closed.

"No."

Something in Soong's tone made him snap open his eyes, and for the first time he noticed that Soong's garments were dusty, and in some places, torn. Never before had Soong appeared before him in such disarray. There must be a very good reason.

"What of these raiders, General?"

"We were able to repulse them without injury to my men. They fled the way they had entered, and I have added guards to the Wall."

"Guards to the Wall . . . I've never heard of such a thing. No one has ever had need to guard the Wall of Living Stone."

"Not until now."

He frowned. Gold Lotus offered him wine, but he waved her aside, indicating she should give some to the general. "But why now?"

"Since the death of your father, Your Majesty, these raids by bandits have increased significantly. Oh, we have always had a stray bandit or two wandering along the outer Wall, but never have they entered the Garden. But they have grown in boldness. They are much fiercer than before, and the rise in incidents greatly disturbs me." He locked his hands behind his back and began pacing.

"A mere coincidence, I would suggest, Your Majesty," the priest said.

Soong whirled, his dark eyes glaring at Villadiego, whose expression remained impassive. "It is no coincidence. I think there is some hidden purpose behind these raids."

The priest lifted an eyebrow. Beside him, Spring Rain shivered, as if she had grown cold all of a sudden. She stepped closer to the emperor.

Ty-Sun beckoned to Never Grieve, who brought a tray of honeyed rice cakes and pistachios to him.

"Must I remind you once more of the prophecy, Your Majesty?"

That again, he thought wearily as he savored a candied orange peel. Soong must make everything tiresome. He closed his eyes, but the old soldier did not notice and continued talking.

"At that time of great joyous celebration throughout the Garden for your illustrious birth an old man from the countryside stepped forward and revealed that he was a sage. Your father invited him to take a meal in celebration, and it was then that the sage foretold the deaths of the Willow Garden and Earth if the dragons were ever destroyed.

"But, the old man said there was a way of saving all. This could be accomplished only if you took an empress from the Outside within three years of the anniversary of your father's death. If you delay so much as a week, all will be lost."

"Yes, yes, I know all of that," Ty-Sun replied impatiently. Really, Soong was getting to be an old fool now. He glanced at the Jesuit and saw his own opinion reflected there. "Have you nothing new to say to me, General?"

"I do, Your Majesty, if you will simply hear me out. I believe that the Willow Garden faces mortal danger from a dark force stirring in the outer world, and that you must act now to avert disaster."

Once more Ty-Sun smiled indulgently. All his life he had lived within the sheltered Garden, and thus his view of life was narrow. And because of his exalted position and the peace that the Garden had always enjoyed, he truly believed that nothing ever could harm him or his kingdom. Why should that happen now, when the Garden had never before faced any disaster?

"And you are suggesting the Garden faces peril . . . based simply on a raid by bandits." Villadiego's voice held scorn, and one of the concubines tittered, then hid her face.

Soong paid no attention to the priest's sarcasm. He believed he knew what his young emperor must be thinking, but he also knew that Ty-Sun, at heart, was a good man, who wished to do only good for his people and for his land. He also knew that, unfortunately, the emperor was the essence of laziness and had been indulged far too much in childhood, while being provided with a multitude of creature comforts. Further, Ty-Sun had never faced any challenge in his short life.

Soong had tried many times—all in vain—to convince the late Emperor that his son should be taught the ways of the warrior, as well as those of the poet and scholar, but Ty-Ch'an had claimed that the Garden was eternally safe from all dangers posed by the outside world. How wrong Ty-Ch'an had been. If he could only convince Ty-Sun of the danger, Soong knew that the young emperor would find strength enough within himself to save the Garden and those who dwelled there.

"I beg you, Your Majesty, please listen to General Soong." It was Spring Rain.

"No more today." With a wave of his hand, he dismissed the old warrior.

"You may regret this," Soong said, then spun about and strode away from the dais.

Ty-Sun frowned slightly as he thoughtfully stroked the fur on Lu's head. "Was that a threat, do you think, Father?"

"I do not think even he would presume as much," Villadiego said in his soft voice, and smiled at Spring Rain, who glanced away.

"Good, good. I would not wish to interpret it as such. It smacks too much of treason and other such unpleasantries. Now, where was I? Was I not about to listen to petitions?"

He glanced at the Upholder of Ceremonies, who leaped forward and bowed so low he needed help in standing straight again.

Only once did Ty-Sun spare a moment to glance at the far end of the hall, but Soong was gone now, and with a slight quirk to his lips, he dismissed any thought of the general from his mind.

5

For the next few days Ty-Sun gave no more thought to Soong's ominous words. After all, there was the Festival of Lively Intellect to think of, and he must write another poem, this having been especially requested by Sheng-mu that very afternoon when she made her regular visit with the other gods.

He had just sat down to his black lacquer writing desk, with a ceramic pot of green tea set to one side, as well as a small platter of candied chrysanthemum petals for when his inspiration faltered. He took up the brush, rubbed it against the block of ink, then paused as he stared off into the distance.

"Your Majesty!" It was Spring Rain and she was slightly out of breath. Her cheeks were bright pink, as though she had run a long distance.

He set his brush down. "Yes?"

"I came as quickly as possible to see if you had heard the latest news?"

He frowned. "News?"

She nodded her head quickly. "Yes. Just this morning a village, located beyond the Wall, was raided, and all of its inhabitants were carried off."

"Impossible. Those villages are under our protection, Spring Rain, as anyone well knows." He picked up his brush. "By the way, on your way out, please send for General Soong."

She nodded, leaving as rapidly as she'd arrived. Ty-Sun stared down at his paper and tried concentrating on forming words, but nothing would come. He continued sitting there until Soong came.

Ty-Sun spoke bluntly. "I have just heard about the village."

Soong said nothing, but instead looked directly into the emperor's eyes.

"All the villagers were carried off? This is correct news? There is no exaggeration in this report, Soong?"

"No, Your Majesty, it is accurate."

"How could it happen?"

"The raiders approached the village under the cover of night, and just as dawn came and the villagers were going to the fields to work, the raiders struck. They burned the village to the ground as well."

He closed his eyes momentarily, then looked at the other man. "Yes, yes, I know what you're thinking, Soong. And I concede that something must be done. You were right. As always."

"Then you admit that you must seek a bride to stop this destruction?"

"Yes."

"You should do it as quickly as possible."

Ty-Sun sighed. "I feared you'd say that."

That afternoon to the complete bewilderment of his chamberlain and ministers, Ty-Sun announced that he would soon be traveling outside the Garden to seek an empress to sit at his side.

"But Your Majesty, have we not fine women within the Garden for you?" asked Quiet Rabbit, the chamberlain. He was a short man, exceedingly roly-poly, with thin arched eyebrows like those of a concubine. It was whispered among some circles at court that Quiet Rabbit was in truth a eunuch. He wore a plum-colored robe with white drakes embroidered along the hem.

"Indeed, we do, Quiet Rabbit, but alas, I cannot marry one from here." His voice held little conviction. "My bride must be from the Outside."

"Your Majesty—" the chamberlain began.

"The prophecy," Ty-Sun said and would say no more on the matter.

Days passed, though, as various preparations were initiated, and still the raids by the as yet unidentified bandits continued, now occurring almost daily. Ty-Sun ordered more men to stand guard on the Wall, but this did little to deter the raiders. And still he moved no closer to leaving. Whenever Soong approached him about a date for departure, Ty-Sun would merely wave casually and smile. Grumbling under his breath, Soong would leave.

Finally, when an entire month had elapsed Soong could tolerate the delay no longer and went directly to someone he knew would be able to do something.

"My lady," he said, bowing low when admitted into Spring Rain's chambers. Her suite was smaller than those of the other concubines, a stipulation she had made on her own, although Ty-Sun would gladly have installed her in quarters nearly as large as his. The room in which Soong stood was decorated in soft colors, and one large window was open to a magnificent view of the rose garden. On a low table alongside the window stood a miniature mountain of malachite, set in a lacquer tray. A large grey cat lay curled in sleep on a cushion.

"General, how good to see you." She put down the poem she had been reading and smiled warmly at him. "How may I help you?"

"I have come to you about an important matter, my lady. I would not have bothered you otherwise—this I think you know."

"Yes."

"But, unfortunately, I have no one else to turn to, no one but you." Prudently she waited. "I have come to ask you to help me persuade the emperor to leave on his journey soon. Despite the increasing number of raids and my advice, he takes this matter altogether too lightly. He delays, believing that he has many months to squander. But he doesn't. It has already been six months since the death of his father. Too much of the time left to him has elapsed already. He must find a wife before the three-year period is up."

She cocked her head to one side. "He has said nothing to me about leaving soon."

Soong sighed heavily. "You see! He doesn't yet believe—he still doesn't fully understand." He paced the room, then faced her once more. "There is the matter of travel, too. The emperor has never been beyond the Wall of Living Stone, and thus he doesn't understand that it will take us months to travel —maybe even as long as a year. An incredibly great distance is involved, and that will take time, perhaps more than we have."

"Have you shown him a map?"

Soong's lips twisted into a wry smile. "I have tried. He pointed out that none of the maps were charted by our people, and thus, were highly unreliable."

"Oh my."

"My thoughts precisely. When I leaned upon my own experiences in the Outside, he merely said I was somewhat prejudiced. And thus, that's why I've come to you now, my lady. You are the only one at the court who is able to persuade him to do anything. He will listen to you—in the end."

"You did not go to Fray Villadiego? I understand he has some influence over the emperor."

"No," Soong said, a frown spreading across his face. "This is a matter of our own people. You carry the most influence over Ty-Sun."

"Very well, General Soong. I understand what must be done, and I will do what I can."

"Without delay, please."

She inclined her head. "I will go to see him this very moment."

Soong helped her to her feet, then bowed and left, again conveying his thanks, but when Spring Rain found Ty-Sun, he was playing chess with the Jesuit priest. She remained bowed until Ty-Sun told her to rise.

"My lord, I must talk to you." She kept her eyes downcast. "Alone."

A faint smile on his lips, he glanced at the priest. "Very well. We will continue our game sometime later, Father."

"As you wish, Your Majesty." The priest rose and bowed to the emperor, then glanced once at the young woman as he left.

"Now, my pet, what is it that you must speak to me about?" He sipped from a goblet carved of pure lapis lazuli and indicated she should sit beside him, which she did promptly. She poured herself some wine, but did not drink.

"It is an important matter, my lord."

"Yes?"

"It is about your departure from the Willow Garden," she replied.

"You will miss me," he suggested playfully.

"Not at all, my lord."

"What?"

She spoke quickly before he formed the wrong opinion. "I will miss you not at all, my lord, because I wish to come with you."

Astonished, he gazed at her. "Come now, my dear, be reasonable. You cannot come with me because we will be faced with an arduous journey. There will even be great dangers." He looked none too pleased at this thought. "And besides, you are a woman."

"I can't deny my sex, my lord, but I am no frail flower. I

have lived a vigorous life, too. And should I remind you, my lord, of your own ancestor—the Empress An, who was a warrior as well?"

"Yes, yes, I know my heritage, but you are not a warrior."

"No, but my father raised my sisters and me with some knowledge of defense."

She was so demure when she spoke that he could hardly believe that she knew how to use a weapon. And yet . . . yet he knew he should never underestimate a woman, particularly Spring Rain.

"Well . . ."

"You will need someone to tend to you and to listen to you, and so all the more reason I should come with you to help ease the way."

He smiled. "You are a minx. Perhaps you are right. Perhaps you should come along." He knew that he would miss her greatly if she remained behind. She was the most beautiful and intelligent of his concubines, and he could talk to her when he couldn't to the others. Each had one or two exceptional qualities; only Spring Rain had many.

"Thank you, my lord, for allowing me to come with you." She waited.

"There is more, Spring Rain?"

"Yes, my lord. It has been nearly six months since your exalted father died."

"And?"

"And because so much time has fled, I beg you to recall the words of the prophecy. You have only three years in which to find an empress. Much time has elapsed, my lord, and I fear more months will fly by while preparations are made. If you are to leave, you must leave soon."

He stroked his chin thoughtfully. "Perhaps you are correct. Perhaps I should. Yes, I will have the work stepped up, done more quickly."

"When do you wish to leave then?"

"I will tell you tomorrow. Today I must think about it. But in the meantime . . ." He smiled, and held out his arms to her.

6

Fray Villadiego asked if he could accompany the emperor on his trip, and Ty-Sun agreed, suspecting he would need some intellectual stimulation on this journey, something Villadiego provided in plenty.

Once he learned that Spring Rain had convinced Ty-Sun to set a departure date, Soong paid another visit and persuaded him—in an effort to trim the time even more—to send messengers ahead announcing their coming. Ty-sun agreed amiably.

"But how will the emperor know the right woman?" Spring Rain asked that evening when the three sat together outside. The sun had just sunk below the West Mountains, and fireflies flitted through the gardens.

"The prophecy says that the woman destined to be empress will be able to call the dragons to her. Thus will she prove she is the right one," Soong said.

"We could bring a dragon along," Ty-Sun suggested after a moment's thought.

"That would be highly impractical," the general said in a dry tone. "It would be dangerous for the creature—not to mention us."

"What about using the dragonleaf?" Spring Rain suggested as she poured wine into the men's goblets. She sat down and looked to General Soong.

The dragonleaf was a sweetly flavored herb upon which the dragons liked to feed, even more than tender bamboo. The creatures had been known to fly thousands of *li* for a mere mouthful of the delicacy.

"There is no other plant more connected with the dragons than dragonleaf, it's true, but I'm not sure that it would work."

"What choice do we have?" Soong asked.

"None, I think."

"Too, would it not be logical that the empress would be able to call to the dragons and have them respond—just as you do, my lord?"

"I hadn't thought of that, Spring Rain."

She flashed a quick smile at Soong, who nodded with satisfaction.

And thus each messenger was supplied with a fair quantity

of dragonleaves and carefully instructed by Ty-Sun in how to employ the herb. If such a woman were found, the envoys were instructed to send a messenger at once to Ty-Sun so that he could come to them. He had also provided each man with a detailed itinerary of his journey. This was Spring Rain's suggestion, and one which Soong greatly approved.

Finally, on the fifth day of the Autumn Moon of the Crane, the frantic preparations ended. General Soong, who had been taking care of military matters, said he and his men would meet Ty-Sun and his entourage on the other side of the East Gate. From there they would turn south toward the seacoast, where Soong had hired boats for their sea voyage.

In a quiet ceremony attended only by those closest to him, Ty-Sun delivered the Star Wand, symbol of his wardship of the dragons, to the care of Quiet Rabbit and, after giving thanks at the Temple of Heaven's Gate and imploring the gods for a fruitful and safe venture, he and his entourage departed the island upon which the imperial city sat and headed eastward into the Wilderness Wood. Ty-Sun was borne in a huge litter of rosewood, trimmed with gold and silver tassels. He wore a robe of red silk, emblazoned with gold imperial dragons, all with five claws, and even his boots were kidskin dyed gold.

Litters carrying his concubines swayed alongside. He had had the unpleasant task of informing Never Grieve, Yeh Tsu-ying and Gold Lotus that they would not be accompanying him, and as he had expected, they did not take the news well. For the past few nights he had been comforting them one by one. They would accompany him only as far as the Wall of Living Stone.

Just before the entourage reached the East Gate, a glow appeared to one side. Ty-Sun ordered a halt, and as he watched, the glow strengthened and became the form of the Princess of Streaked Clouds. Sheng-mu stepped forward and greeted him.

"Good day to you, Your Highness. Have you come to travel with us?"

"No, Ty-Sun, but I have brought you a gift." She handed him something wrapped in cloth.

He quickly pulled off the gold cloth to find a cylinder of clear glass in his hands. Inside were hundreds of tiny fire pearls. As he raised the glass, all of the pearls rose to the top.

"Thank you," he said slowly, not sure what the gift was.

Sheng-mu saw his confusion. "It is a time-telling glass. A

pearl will drop for each day that passes, and thus you will be able to keep track of the time left to you."

"Ah, I see now. Thank you." He handed it to one of the servants, who placed it carefully in the sandalwood box attached to Ty-Sun's litter.

"Now, I must go. Good-bye, Ty-Sun." She bowed, then looked across at Spring Rain and smiled at the young girl, who bowed her head in response.

The goddess disappeared as quickly as she'd appeared, and Ty-Sun bade farewell to his three weeping concubines, waved to Quiet Rabbit, and ordered his men to open the great gate.

From a position on a slight rise just beyond the Wall of Living Stone, General Soong and his men, astride the fast and hardy ponies that served as their warhorses, waited none too patiently. He had drawn some of his best men from his two divisions, the west which was the White Tiger, and the east, the Green Snake, to go with them on this journey, and then had left his second-in-command in charge of the army.

He was tired of waiting, and so were the men and the horses. Beneath him his pony stomped its feet, its hooves ringing on the rock, and he leaned down and patted its shaggy neck. He shifted in the leather saddle, then sighed with relief as the immense gates to the Land of Ten Thousand Willows were pulled slowly open and the entourage started pouring through to the Outside.

It was about time, Soong thought. Ty-Sun was an hour overdue.

And the entourage kept streaming through the gates. Minute after minute, with no apparent end in sight. Soong's eyes narrowed as he watched. He had instructed Ty-Sun not to bring much because they would travel faster if packed lightly. As usual, it looked as if Ty-Sun had ignored his suggestion.

Just at casual glance, Soong saw at least five cooks with their entire kitchen staff, fully a dozen wardrobe attendants, not to mention the Grand Usher, the Grand Coachman, an entire flank of household guards, half his normal number of advisors with their assistants and servants, several dozen page boys and messengers, imperial grooms, a gardener, a troupe of musicians and singers, the emperor's favorite actor, and of course, his old tutor—doubtless, Soong thought sarcastically, to read poetry to the emperor late at night when he could not sleep. It was a long-established tradition.

Surely that was close to three hundred people, and it was about two hundred and fifty too many. He would speak with Ty-Sun as soon as he could.

Ty-Sun's people had no sooner reached Soong's soldiers than a shrill cry split the morning air. Immediately Soong's hand went to his long bow and he began shouting orders.

"What is it?" Ty-Sun asked, bewildered by the sudden activity. "What's going on, General?" He heard the cry again.

Weapons out and ready, Ty-Sun's household guards circled the imperial litter. Ch'u, whom Ty-Sun had brought for additional company, began barking as the entire entourage was surrounded by dark men, who had swooped down out of the low hills in front of them. Soong and his men jumped forward to meet the bandits, who were outnumbered two to one.

Ty-Sun watched with fascination as the general raised his long bow and let loose an arrow. With a singing sound, the arrow found its target in the chest of a bandit, who pitched forward. The other soldiers slashed at the bandits with swords and daggers, and soon, seeing that their cause was lost, those bandits not killed fled back into the hills.

"That was close," Ty-Sun breathed as Soong rode back toward him. The general's clothes were a little dusty, and he had a slight scratch along one cheek, but other than that he hadn't been touched. At present his men were quickly burying the dead bandits so they could get going; none of his warriors had fallen in the fray, thank the gods.

Ty-Sun shuddered, and felt the immediate need for some icy wine. Overhead a flock of black birds passed, their shadow touching him. He glanced toward them, then away, feeling suddenly chilled.

Soong shot him an amused look. "That wasn't even a hard battle, Your Majesty. They were simply testing our strength."

"Oh."

"And that," Soong continued, grimly this time, "is why I did not want you to travel so heavily. We would be better able to defend ourselves, if the entourage were far smaller. I doubt that next time we will be so lucky to be without casualties."

"Smaller?" Ty-Sun exclaimed. "I cannot do without my people; all of them are most necessary. I could not live without each and every one."

Soong grimaced. "I grant you some are needed, Your Majesty. But surely you can dispense with some services this one time."

"All are necessary." A stubborn look transformed the emperor's features.

"Extravagance, sheer extravagance," the general muttered, but no matter what he said he could not convince Ty-Sun to trim the party.

That night when they made camp for the evening Soong asked to see Ty-Sun's agenda.

"I don't have one," he replied.

"But I thought you had supplied your envoys with one when they set out."

"Well, yes, I did."

"Then let me see that one."

"There's too much traveling involved, Soong. I don't want to be away for the entire three years, you know." Even as he spoke, he glanced over at the glass cylinder and a tiny fire pearl slowly fell. The first day of his journey was finished.

"You must travel wherever you think you might find your bride, Your Majesty," the general replied diplomatically.

"I had thought to travel about the East. Perhaps to Japan or India, perhaps Burma or Laos."

Soong and Spring Rain exchanged looks, both knowing why Ty-Sun considered only the East: the Garden was closer to these countries. Thus he wouldn't have to travel as much. Soong, also, knew, or rather suspected, that an empress would not be found there. A hunch told him that the empress lived in the West, a notion that made much sense to him. An emperor from the East, an empress from the West, and with the melding of the two, the melding of the two halves of the world, and thus its ultimate salvation.

Soong remained silent.

"Do you have objections to these countries?" Ty-Sun's tone was slightly peevish.

Soong shrugged casually. "The Lao people are descended from the Tai family of China long ago, but since then there has been much intermingling of blood. Too, the Burmese rule the country at this time."

"I will go to Burma then, because it is a forceful nation."

"Yes, I'm quite sure you could approach the Toungoo dynasty, but I understand their people are fierce by nature. I don't think you would wish a bloodthirsty empress."

"After the birth of your son," Spring Rain said, "she might slip in one night and cut your throat."

Ty-Sun paled, then shook his head. "Japan? It is much

closer to us, and in many ways similar to the Willow Garden."

Soong had his answer ready immediately. "Iemitsu Tokugawa is shogun, and rules his land with an iron hand. The shadow of the Willow Garden stretches across to his island kingdom, and I do not think he would be satisfied to remain there."

"He would lay siege to the Garden?"

Soong stroked his moustache. "I think it extremely likely, Your Majesty. Remember, Tokugawa's reign is essentially a military dictatorship."

"Oh my." Ty-Sun sighed heavily. "Then what of India? Surely, I could find an empress there. The Indians have an old culture, as we do."

"Yes," Soong replied grimly, "Shah Jahan, the current Mughal emperor, had his elder brother strangled so that he could ascend to the throne, and then once he ascended to the throne had his father-in-law murder the other royal princes so they would pose no threat."

"Oh my," Ty-Sun echoed again. "Then he might have me murdered."

"Precisely, and he would rule in your stead. With the combined land—and wealth—of the Willow Garden and India, few could stand before him.

"I think you must look much farther beyond the boundaries of the East."

"The West. Only that is left."

"Indeed."

"But the West . . . it's so completely alien to us. It scarcely has a civilization worth thinking . . . much less speaking . . . of."

"Remember, Your Majesty, that many of the dragons came originally from the West."

"But it was the West that drove them out," Ty-Sun countered.

"Some less understanding souls existed in the West, perhaps, but that has been many years ago, too. Doubtless they have changed greatly. Too, the West would bring new blood, fresh ideas to the Garden."

"Doubtless," Ty-Sun murmured, although he did not look entirely convinced. "Of course, my old friend, you are better traveled than I. Perhaps you are correct. I will consider what you have said, Soong." He yawned. "Until tomorrow then. What time do we leave?"

"We must rise early tomorrow and so cannot linger to have a long breakfast," he added, with a meaningful look at the emperor's waistline.

"Early? When is that?"

"Before the sun rises, Your Majesty."

"That's still part of the night."

"Be that as it may, we must leave then. We cannot delay."

"Very well," the emperor said with a long-suffering sigh. "Spring Rain, come with me. I think I wish to hear your soothing voice."

"Very well, Your Majesty."

Soong bowed, turned and left the emperor to his thoughts of an all too short night.

7

Several days later the emperor's enormous entourage reached the coast, and there they boarded the junks Soong had commandeered earlier. What he had not anticipated were all the additional members of the imperial household, so he was forced to secure several more junks, smaller this time, to accommodate the overflow.

Soong would be aboard *The Phoenix* when not with Ty-Sun, while Ty-Sun took *The Water Dragon* as his flagship. The other ships were *The Partridge Sky, The Moth, The Hummingbird, The Red Willow Dream*, and *The Jade Butterfly*. If the ships ever moved out of range of the voice, Soong had ordered pigeons caged aboard the ships to send messages.

The junks were constructed of camphorwood, with exquisite teakwood decks and masts, magnificent red and gold sails sewn of an exceptionally hardy silk, and fittings of polished brass. The trim around the ports was painted black, and Ty-Sun thought they looked like eyes lined with kohl. The hulls were painted gold, and each ship bore an intricately carved figurehead.

Ty-Sun smiled at the largest boat, which would be his. The figurehead was an impressive dragon, its mouth open in a silent roar. He approved heartily. *The Phoenix* had a painted bird on its keel, and the other boats possessed special emblems too. Above Ty-Sun's ship flew a standard of red with a gold dragon upon it.

Each junk could comfortably carry seventy passengers or more, in addition to the crew. Soong grumbled to himself about having a fleet of seven ships now instead of the three he'd wanted, but there was nothing he could do yet. Perhaps along the way Ty-Sun would send some of these people back.

Once the ships were ready to sail, Ty-Sun's ministers made an appearance.

"You must go south," counseled Tsay-hua, Ty-Sun's head minister. A Citizen of the First Rank, he wore a ruby ring, and had a stork embroidered on the back and breast of his robe.

"Yes, yes, Your Majesty, you must order the ship southward," chimed in Sheu-kee, his second minister, his head nodding ridiculously fast so that the long jade drop earrings he wore jangled musically. "Not, of course, that we are *telling*

Your Majesty what he must do, because he is, after all, the exalted emperor while we are only lowly servants of His Majesty."

Tuu-dow nodded, then spoke in his too-soft voice. "It is true, Your Majesty, we would never presume to tell Your Majesty what to do, nor would we stay Your Majesty's hand from the course which he wishes to follow. Furthermore, we would presume—"

"Enough of this silliness!" Soong roared. "We must sail northward, Your Majesty, because far greater speed is possible in that direction."

"But the Great Ice lies there," quavered Sheu-kee, as his eyes fell quickly before the stern look of the old general. His pudgy lower lip trembled and he twisted the hem of his long sleeve. He was a Citizen of the Second Rank and wore a silk robe embroidered with a golden pheasant. His rings nearly disappeared in the rolls of fat on his hands.

Tuu-dow nodded. "Your Majesty, it would be certain death to attempt to negotiate the Great Ice. Certain death," he squeaked.

"Why yes, it would be," Tsay-hua said with a nervous look to the old soldier. "While we must acknowledge the many years of service General Soong has given Your Majesty, it must be pointed out that . . ."

"Pointed out that what?" Soong asked in a reasonable tone of voice.

"Nothing."

"I thought not." Soong looked to Ty-Sun. "I admit, Your Majesty, that there could be some danger, but it is not certain death as these . . . butterflies . . . would have you imagine."

Ty-Sun smiled benevolently. "I think that you are to be trusted in this matter, Soong. We will go northward." His smile broadened at the stricken looks upon the faces of his three ministers. "Rest assured, gentlemen—must I remind you that I can command the Gods to come to me? We have no fear of any ice, great or otherwise." He chuckled, a relaxed sound.

More reassured now, the three ministers smiled and looked at each other with congratulatory expressions, almost as if they had suggested the idea of sailing north themselves.

Soong sighed, thinking it would be a very long trip.

As the junks sailed northward, the air grew increasingly frigid. Spring Rain, wrapped in a cloak lined in marmoset fur, stepped out onto the deck and found Soong leaning against the railing, gazing out into the dark blue waters.

"It's so cold," she said, shivering slightly as she tucked her hands into the sleeves of her robe.

"Yes, and it will only grow colder from now on." Slivers of frost dotted Soong's moustache, and his breath steamed when he spoke. "We'll have to start lighting the braziers at night and keep them tended at all times. I don't want any of the ships catching fire."

"You've kept your armor on."

"I decided to wear it from now on. I don't like how we were caught unaware just as we stepped out of our own land."

He would not be caught off guard again like that, he told himself. He wore brigandine, black velvet lined with small iron plates fastened with rivets with gilded heads. The shoulder pieces were shaped like gilded dragons with four claws, for only the emperor could wear dragons with five.

Ivory buttons fastened the shoulder and arm pieces together, while the helmet with raised designs decorating it, cuffs and kneeguards, were steel inlaid with gold. His boots were black leather with heavy cord soles. He also wore *hu sin king*, or mirror guarding heart, circular plates of white metal with ornamental borders, worn across the breast and the back of his armor. Under his armor he wore a plain black tunic and trousers that ended just above his ankles.

The armored bow case of jazerant with velvet bands and long blue fringe contained whistling arrows over four feet in length. Because their large hollow heads had openings in the front, the arrows filled with air when released and thus whistled during their flight. His bow of bamboo was well over five and a half feet long, and had a pull of nearly two hundred pounds.

Even though the armor weighed more than his usual clothing, Soong moved as agilely as if he wore nothing but a silk robe. His step was just as light as before.

"Is it as dangerous as they say?" the concubine asked softly.

Soong knew whom she meant. "It is dangerous, but Tsayhua and the others would make the emperor fear to rise in the morning, if they had their way. They shouldn't have been brought along. There were other men of far greater courage whom we could have used; certainly this is not a journey for the fainthearted."

"No, I think not."

"Will you fare well?" Soong asked, turning his head to look at his small companion.

She smiled. "Have you not forgotten, General Soong? I am the daughter of peasants. I am no stranger to hardships, and I will stand against all that comes, for the sake of my lord."

"Well spoken, little one. Now, come below, and let us have some warm plum wine to take away the chill."

Ty-Sun watched as General Soong and Spring Rain left the deck, and he stepped out from where he had stood concealed behind the spar. He hadn't wanted to reveal himself, because both of them, in their different ways, would fuss over him. They meant well, he knew, and he knew also he was lucky to have them both watching over him, but tonight he wanted to be alone.

He leaned against the railing, feeling the coldness of the teak against his skin, and glanced upward into the vastness of the sky. Even this far north, he could still see the constellations of the Purple Exaltation, the Eunuch's Star, the Emperor's Throne, and the Seats of the Ministers. And there, among moon-laurels and star-elms, were Herd-Boy Star and Heavenly River Maid, always fixed in their positions to the south and north of the River of Silver. The two lovers were destined to meet, or so the legend went, only once a year on the seventh day of the seventh lunar month. On that day magpies build a bridge for the lovers to cross.

He smiled. If only it were so simple. He chuckled aloud now. If only he could wave his hands, or Dragon's Tongue . . . or something . . . and his bride-to-be would be there. Was he not a sorcerer? Why could he not produce her by means of magic?

He wondered what this woman would be like. Would she like him? Could she grow to love him in time? Would he love her, or would she simply be the woman who sat at his side, who advised him, who bore his daughters and sons? A great sadness welled up within him at the thought. He hoped she would not simply perform her duties by rote; he wanted her to be more. He wanted his bride to share his thoughts and his likes, and even his dislikes, to be able to go walking with him across Nine Dragon Bridge without any fear and feel welcomed in that special place among his friends.

He wanted too much, he suspected, and pushed away from

the railing. Enough of this sobering thought. He was stiff from the cold, and he would go below to have something warm. And perhaps later in the night, he would bring Spring Rain into bed with him, and she would hold him as she had done many other times.

As he went across to the hatch, he did not see the shadow that slid across the deck, then stopped short of the hatch. It watched for a few more minutes, then slowly dissipated.

8

The following day Ty-Sun found the old general alone once more upon the deck. Even though still fairly early in the day, the sunlight was dim, as though it were near nightfall. Ty-Sun, glancing up, could scarcely see the sun; it shone faintly, as though many layers of clouds lay in between, and yet the sky wasn't cloudy.

Soong glanced briefly at him, then turned back to stare at the icy waters. His face was drawn, and there were circles under his eyes.

"Did you sleep last night?" Ty-Sun demanded, thrusting his hands inside the full sleeves of his robe. He shivered at the cold. The air was more raw than the day before and he wished he hadn't hurried out, clad in nothing heavier than his robes.

"No, I wanted to keep watch, Your Majesty."

"Then you must sleep now."

"I must stay up here, I need to stay awake, Your Majesty. I sense something. . . ." He shrugged, unable to put into words what he felt.

Ty-Sun, too, had been uneasy through the night. He had awakened while it was still dark outside, and he had thought he had seen a shadow move alongside his bed, but when he sat up, no one was there. The uneasiness had increased so much that he had been unable to sleep. Had he known Soong was above deck he would have joined him much earlier.

"Do you sense danger?"

Soong shrugged. He wasn't sure what he felt, only that he needed to watch. For what, he didn't know.

Overhead a flock of large black birds screamed against the wind, which had risen steadily since Ty-Sun had come on deck. The birds were the first living creatures he had seen since he and his entourage came aboard the junks a few days before.

Ever so slowly the great ship, its six sisters in its wake, nudged through the freezing water. Sometimes the junk moved so slowly that Ty-Sun thought it had come to a standstill. On all sides of the ships loomed mountainous icebergs, taller than the most impressive temple in the Willow Garden, while bitter winds blew across the deck. It seemed that they faced an impenetrable wall of ice. The water was growing thicker, more ice than liquid now, while the increasing strength of the wind made further conversation impossible. So they simply stood and stared out in the whiteness ahead of them, to the sides, behind them.

Ty-Sun felt himself slipping into a dreamlike state, but he couldn't stop it. All he could see in front of him was white, dazzling white sunlight glinting off snow and ice, and he was blinded. Something large, something dark, something menacing swooped down out of the sky. He flinched when something soft touched his arm. He whirled around.

It was Spring Rain and in her hands she held a fur cloak for him. He could see the concern in her eyes and knew she wanted to stay with him, but it was too cold and so he sent her below. Then Soong touched his arm and pointed ahead of the ship.

All was white now.

"It's no good," Soong shouted above the howling wind. "We're losing too much time with this ice. Had we left a few months . . . even weeks . . . earlier, we would not have met with such resistance so soon."

"That's my fault. And I'll soon rectify it." He clapped his hand, but no servant could hear and so he went to the hatch and ordered a page to bring him his sword, Dragon's Tongue.

"What do you intend to do?"

Ty-Sun smiled mysteriously. "Call up some of your men, Soong."

Within minutes a score of Soong's men presented themselves to the emperor.

"Stand back!" he cried, lifting Dragon's Tongue with both hands. The sword was ancient, a relic from the emperor who had founded the Willow Garden thousands of years ago, and it was long, over four feet. Made of tempered steel, Dragon's Tongue was smooth, completely devoid of any runes along its fine, slightly curved blade. Its golden hilt was shaped like the head of a dragon and to put one's hand through the hilt was to place it in the mouth of the beast.

Ty-Sun slammed the sword sideways into the nearest chunk of ice alongside the junk, and the sword sliced through it as though it were nothing more than an overripe peach. Blue sparks flew from the metal as he brought the sword down across the ice once more.

"Follow the emperor's example!" Soong cried as he realized what Ty-Sun was doing.

Soon the soldiers were hacking away at the ice, gradually

freeing a narrow path through which the junks could sail. Ty-Sun would attack the ice first because his sword could do more damage initially, then the soldiers would take up his abandoned position and hack the bergs into smaller pieces.

Watching the beads of sweat roll from his emperor's face with each blow of the mighty sword, Soong smiled wryly. The Ty-Sun of only a week ago would not have done this labor. The Ty-Sun of a week ago would have fled below deck at the first thought of work he must do himself. Perhaps some good would come out of this journey, after all, Soong thought.

But even as the men worked, they began faltering as a dank fog rolled in, obscuring sight of all ice. Suddenly Ty-Sun cupped his hand to his ear.

"Do you hear that?" he shouted over the wail of the wind.

"Hear what?" the general began, then stopped as he, too, heard something beyond the winds. Something almost like . . . voices.

Unearthly voices rose around them in the moist darkness, and Ty-Sun and Soong turned this way and that, seeking the source. As the volume of the alluring voices increased, the decks grew crowded with ministers and page boys and cooks, and other members of the imperial household who wished to discover the source.

Then, through a break in the fog, Ty-Sun saw the creatures calling to him and to his people. Reclining on ice floes, the singers were of human shape, men and women alike, but there the resemblance stopped. They had the faces of fish with wide gaping mouths and round cold eyes.

Horrified, he turned away, yet the seductive voices continued calling to him. He heard them call him by name. He started toward the railing when Soong's hand clamped down hard on his arm. The touch of the other man shook him from the enchantment.

"Look," Soong said, pointing.

Several of the creatures had slipped off of their beds of ice and were swimming toward the junks.

Soong's face was ashen as he turned to look at Ty-Sun. "If those things come on board, they'll destroy us, Your Majesty. We must do something at once."

Ty-Sun heard a sudden splash and whirling around saw minister Sheu-kee disappear over the side of *The Water Dragon.* An assistant to one of the cooks followed, as did several grooms and a little servant girl. The other ships were losing passengers just as rapidly, too. He could no longer delay.

He held his arms up to the leaden sky and took a deep breath, confident in his ability. "Hear my words, O Mighty Erh-lang. Come speedily with your companion, the Celestial Dog, to aid us in our great time of need. Come to us, I beg you."

Ty-Sun waited, knowing that the god's appearance might take a moment or so, but when several minutes passed and nothing happened, he frowned. In the past when he had invoked the god, the Second Lord had appeared almost at once; the same with any god or goddess. Always they had come when he beckoned. Was he not the Son of Heaven, always to be obeyed?

Puzzled, he repeated his words, louder this time in case the god had not heard the earlier invocation, but once again Erh-lang did not appear.

Soong grappled with a half-fish creature, who was nearly over the railing. Finally, he stabbed the thing in the chest with his dagger and pushed it away, then grabbed the robe of a young man who was about to go overboard.

The air was filled with agonized screams as those in the water were attacked by the singing creatures. The icy water became a bubbling red whirlpool, as man after man disappeared beneath the churning surface.

"I have no choice," Ty-Sun said softly, as though to himself, and as Soong leaped forward with his long crossbow and began twanging arrows, Ty-Sun wielded Dragon's Tongue. The scene was the same across the seven decks: soldiers and guards fought the terrible things that inched up the sides of the ship. The decks grew slippery underfoot from the blood of the wounded and dying.

Ty-Sun swung his sword as a fishman, its round eyes staring unblinkingly, rushed toward him, and when the sword sliced through the thing's flesh, a foul-smelling blood spurted onto his face and cloak. Some splashed onto his lips, and his stomach turned at its putrid taste. He wiped it away with his sleeve.

He slew creature after creature, while their number seemed endless. Just as he killed one, another was there to replace it. His arm was tiring, the muscles beginning to burn from exertion, for he was unaccustomed to holding the heavy sword for very long, and it seemed as if he had been fighting for hours.

The sound of battle continued around the emperor, and

when at last he risked a quick look at Soong, he saw that the old general was all right. Even as Ty-Sun watched, Soong nocked another arrow and let it loose. It found its target in the eye of a half-fish thing clambering over the railing, and with a thin shriek the creature fell back into the water. It was unnerving, but Ty-Sun had noticed that these foes made no sound, beyond the strange singing and their death cry.

Finally, hours later, the attack ended and the last handful of creatures slipped off their ice floes and swam away from the ships.

Exhausted, Ty-Sun let Dragon's Tongue down so that its tip rested at an angle. The great sword was painted with the foul blood of the fishman. Almost too weary to raise his head, he forced himself to do so and surveyed the deck.

Bodies of the creatures, already smelling like rotting fish, slumped across the bodies of the men he and Soong had lost. Red blood, and blood the color of ichor mingled and ran across the deck. Dull scales, stripped from the creatures' heads, clung here and there, or were gripped in the fists of the dead men. He saw Soong standing only a few feet away and thought the general looked unharmed. Ty-Sun thanked the gods for that, at least.

The ship lurched suddenly, and his stomach heaved at the awful smell and the sight, and he turned toward the sea, gasping for air. Ty-Sun had never seen men killed before, and had certainly never imagined it like this. He closed his eyes tight and wished with all his might that he might be home in his gentle Garden, away from this carnage.

Something dark stirred in the shadows, and Soong's hand went to his bow, but he relaxed when he saw that it was Fray Villadiego.

The priest nodded to them, then threaded his way among the dying, kneeling at their sides to give them the last rites, or murmuring prayers in Latin over the injured men. Soong turned back to Ty-Sun.

Blood and dirt streaked Ty-Sun's handsome face, and his eyes were red-rimmed with exhaustion. Tears inched down his cheeks, only to freeze in the icy air.

"We have lost so many," he murmured, staring sadly around him. "So many."

"But not as many as we might have," Soong replied gruffly. He raised an arm and wiped it across his face. The smell of fish seemed to permeate his clothes, his very skin, and he shuddered. It would be a long time before he would dine on fish again.

Ty-Sun heaved a great sigh. "At least we triumphed over those things. But, I don't understand why Erh-lang and the Celestial Dog did not come to me. They've never failed me before. Never."

"I don't either, Your Majesty. But it's apparent that we can't depend upon their giving us aid." Ty-Sun nodded. "But I wasn't surprised by this attack." He saw the other lift his eyebrows. "As I had suspected, the evil force that waits for us has watched over our journey from the Willow Garden. And it sent these unholy creatures to stop us."

"I saw black birds shortly before the attack, and another flock a few days ago."

Soong nodded. "Spies, I have no doubt."

"Then what are we to do?"

"Delay no further."

Ty-Sun nodded, knowing that the general was correct, then slowly he picked up Dragon's Tongue and moved heavily and clumsily across the deck. He could no longer stand the carnage.

Soong remained above deck to help his men, while Spring Rain and some of the unhurt servants knelt among the wounded, tending their injuries.

They all slept well that night, although Soong doubled the watch on each ship. And when within four days' time the worst of the Great Ice was past, and when no other creature had attacked them, the general's optimism expanded slightly.

And with Soong's advice, Captain Tang aimed the great ship west and south toward Russland.

9

Only a few days later *The Water Dragon* and its companions docked in the northern coastal town of Archangel. They were in Russland now, General Soong informed them as they disembarked. Ty-Sun cared little which country it was; he was simply relieved at having firm ground under his feet once more.

The natives stared at the people from the Willow Garden as though they were beings from some other world. And in a way they were, Spring Rain thought, as she compared the Russlanders' clothing to their own exquisite silk and satin robes. The Russlanders who clustered around the imperial camp were bulky creatures, owing no doubt to the thick dark furs swathing them so completely that male could not be distinguished from female until one saw the long beards on the round faces of the men. Yet the furs were necessary because snow and ice covered everything as far as the eye could see.

The Russlanders spoke a curious language, exceedingly harsh to her ears, and only Soong was able to communicate with them. Spring Rain knew that he had traveled extensively as a youth and had brought back to the Willow Garden a wide knowledge of foreign tongues.

Soong and Ty-Sun found transportation easily and arranged to go to Muscovy, site of the Romanov tsar's court. Only the emperor, Soong, Fray Villadiego and a handful of the surviving ministers would be going; the others would remain aboard the junks.

Departure was set for early the next morning and as Spring Rain watched Ty-Sun enter her small quarters, she thought that he looked somewhat slimmer. The battle with the ice creatures had been fierce and had taxed him; the use of magic was no easy thing, too. He came over to her, then dropped down on the bed and placed his head in her lap. She stroked his forehead, and within minutes he was fast asleep.

Early the next day, when the sky was still a dark grey, the travelers were up and ready to leave. Soong noted with satisfaction that Ty-Sun had not grumbled about rising early, something which would have been unthinkable for him a mere month ago. He smiled, then led the others to their transportation, which turned out to be gaudily painted sleighs pulled by three horses whose coats were thick and long.

"These sleighs are called troikas," Soong informed Ty-Sun and the others, "and they work very well here in this land of snow and ice."

The dour coachmen snapped their whips. The horses tossed their heads, and with the tinkling of dozens of tiny bells sewn on the harnesses, the travelers set off, amidst applause and cheering from those left behind. Fray Villadiego closed his eyes and settled down under his fur lap robe, as if he had done this sort of thing many times before.

Ty-Sun knew he should rest, because he was still tired from the battle, but he couldn't sleep. He was too intrigued by the new sights around him. As the troikas rushed through the dense forests south of Archangel, Ty-Sun wondered what he would find at the Romanov court. Would he find his bride, his only true empress?

Before his father died so unexpectedly, Ty-Sun had thought he might be allowed to marry for love, but now things were different. He had no time to fall in love with a prospective bride; now he would have to find one, marry her, and then see if love were possible, like his parents who had been married for many years before they grew to love one another. If love did not come, well, he would still have his concubines.

The young emperor gazed at the immense trees that towered about them on all sides and thought how gloomy and threatening the woods were. They were nothing like the Imperial Hunting Forest or the Wilderness Wood of his own land, forests where he was comfortable. He felt as if there were things, dark unseen things, in those woods, watching him.

Shivering slightly, he pulled the lap robe up to his chin and forced himself to relax. Ever so slowly his eyes closed and he slept again. Soon he would be meeting Mikhail Feodorovich Romanov, Tsar and Autocrat of All the Russlands.

After three days of almost constant travel in bitter winds and freezing temperatures past frozen rivers and lakes and cloud-peaked mountains, with very little rest, Ty-Sun caught his first glimpse of the hilltop city when it was yet a great distance away, with the light from the weak sun glinting off the gilded cupolas and steeples of the many churches.

Rising above the town was the Kremlin, its red brick walls some sixty-five feet high and almost half that thick. This was the tsar's palace, a walled fortress, possessing some nine churches within its confines. The heavy golden dome belonged to Uspenskii Cathedral, home to most of Russland's sacred relics. Here the tsars were traditionally crowned. To its east the white shaft of the great Bell Tower of Ivan the Great thrust upward into the bleak sky. From it, a watchman could see as far as twenty miles in every direction, as well as watch the winding ribbon that was the Muskovy River. Then there were the dozen domes and spires of the Cathedral of St. Vassili the Blessed.

Upon closer inspection he was somewhat disappointed, having expected a far greater city than he found. Every building, single story or otherwise, was constructed of wood, an item the Russlanders did not lack. Soong told him that the Russlanders disdained the use of stone, fearing that evil spirits occupied it.

A superstitious lot, the tired emperor thought with some irritability, and wondered what other follies he would find.

The city lay without any pattern that he could perceive, beyond being built in ever-increasing walled circles. Its sometimes exceedingly narrow streets twisted this way and that, or back upon themselves, making a virtual maze.

With the closeness of the all-wooden buildings, fire was a great and frequent hazard, and Soong commented that the Russland capital city had been burned down many times in the past century, only to be doggedly rebuilt by the Muscovites. Generally, the streets were muddy, where much traffic traveled them, or deeply snow-covered where few ventured, and many men—there were few women about—walked or went on horseback or rode in sleighs through the streets. Ty-Sun noticed the large number of foreigners, many of them obviously from the West, and thought that a good sign.

The troikas drove through the center of the city to the Kremlin, and the great wooden gates were pulled back to admit them into Red Square. They were left at a small palace, its towers topped with onion-shaped domes, and there given quarters.

As Ty-Sun and Soong walked through the numerous rooms, all quite generous in size, they noted that nearly every wall and ceiling was a deep red. Religious paintings, which Soong called ikons, covered much of the walls. Ty-Sun had no complaints with the servants he was given, nor with the food, nor with the comfort of his bed, a delight to rest in after the sparseness of the ship's bunk.

And there he waited impatiently for three more days before being summoned to Terem Palace.

The three palaces of the tsar were connected by small gardens, elaborate terraces and covered passageways, and were a maze of low corridors, tiny rooms and immense chambers. Bright designs covered every inch of the walls with pictures of mythical beasts, vines and flowers. The throne room and reception room were approached by narrow, well-guarded staircases, on which only two or three men could pass abreast.

Ty-Sun, with Soong and the others following a few steps behind, strode into the room, then stopped as he stared at it. An immense ikon of the Virgin, and one of the Savior, hung behind the throne, while Biblical scenes decorated the red walls.

On either side of the throne stood tall, bearded warriors, dressed in high white fur caps and white kaftans of velvet. They carried shining axes. Nearby were the *boyars*, or nobles, dressed all in gold, while beyond them were roughly dressed men with long moustaches and shaved heads. Cossacks, Soong called them, and said they were nomadic warriors.

As for the throne itself . . . Ty-Sun could not help but stare at its incredible barbaric beauty. He had never seen anything so ugly yet compelling. Set somewhat above the floor so that the tsar could look down upon his court and those who came before him, the huge throne gleamed with jewels. Thousands of gems—diamonds and rubies and pearls and others Ty-Sun could not name—set in gold which had been applied painstakingly by hand over an ancient wood. Steps lined with red velvet led up to the dais.

It was only after his eyes had become less dazed that Ty-Sun noticed the throne's occupant.

Mikhail Feodorovich Romanov was a fairly small man, slight of frame, although that was not particularly noticeable while he sat in state on the throne. He had dark eyes and dark, short-cropped hair, a long nose, a small mouth, and a neatly trimmed moustache and beard. He was not handsome, although not particularly unpleasant-looking, either. He wore a silk crown, rimmed with sable and surmounted by rubies and emeralds the size of pigeon eggs and carried a diamond-studded orb and the golden Muscovite scepter. Exquisite black fur trimmed his ankle-length robes of gold.

In 1613, Soong had told Ty-Sun, after Russland had faced

many years of civil unrest known as the Time of Troubles, Mikhail had been crowned tsar at age sixteen. Prior to that time, his family had been scattered, many living primitively in the forests. He and his mother, who had been forced to become a nun, were brought back from exile by the *boyars*, and it was only years later that he was able to ransom back his own aged father, now a monk.

At the tsar's feet on a three-legged stool sat a tiny man, a dwarf, dressed in miniature robes identical to his master's. The dwarf appeared fairly young, although his features were misshapen, and in his hands he waved a thin scepter like the tsar's. While the man was horrible to look at, Ty-Sun thought, he noticed that the other's eyes were shrewd. The dwarf saw that Ty-Sun was looking at him and glared.

Mikhail smiled at his new guests, then spoke in a resonant voice, with Soong quickly translating for Ty-Sun and the others.

"His Majesty graciously welcomes us to his court, and says that he wishes heartily to help you in your mission however he may."

Ty-Sun inclined his head. "Tell him thank you, and I know that my stay here will be profitable. Now, let him know that we have presents for him."

The dwarf stuck his tongue out, and momentarily Ty-Sun was taken aback. He decided he would simply ignore the creature.

The tsar clapped his hands like a child at this announcement, with the dwarf doing the same, and two of Ty-Sun's ministers brought forth the gifts—bolts of finely spun silk, chests of aromatic spices and incenses, screens of sandalwood, statues in jade and ebony and ivory and coral, caskets containing strings of pearls, a sweetly singing nightingale in a cage of bamboo, similarly two capering monkeys, eggs that when split open spilled yolks that were tiny polished yellow gems, and many more. It was obvious to Ty-Sun that his presents had found great favor in Tsar Mikhail's eyes.

The Tsar appointed one of his most trusted chamberlains as their guide, and the guide, a stocky man with the long beard beloved of the Russlanders, introduced himself as Dmitri Ivanovich Raskonikov. He spoke a little of their language, having, he explained quite buoyantly, learned it from a merchant who had traveled west from the Garden.

Leaving Fray Villadiego with a few of the Orthodox priests

who spoke passable Latin so that they might discuss the merits of each other's religion, Raskonikov escorted Ty-Sun and Soong from the audience chamber and gave them a rather sweeping tour of the three palaces. Then, when it was quite late, he returned them to the banqueting hall, where a feast had been laid out in honor of the visitors from the Willow Garden.

At last they were seated at the long table with Ty-Sun at the tsar's left. The emperor turned to Soong who was next to him and spoke in an undertone so that no one else might overhear. "What do you think so far, General?"

"I think the Russlanders are a barbaric people, as we thought, Your Majesty, although they seem to enjoy life with a great zest. They also seem to be most sincere, although crude in many ways."

"Yes. But what of the women? I haven't seen a single one so far."

"Nor I," Soong admitted, stroking his moustache. He caught Raskonikov's attention across the table. "Tell me, if you can—where are the women? In the palaces that we went through today, we saw no women."

Raskonikov grinned, his jagged teeth shining in the candlelight. "Nor will you, General Soong. The women live in the *terem*."

"But we were in the Terem," Soong said, slightly confused.

Raskonikov nodded sagely. "Ah, but that was the Terem, which is the palace, and I am talking about the *terem*, which are the upper apartments where the women stay."

"Of course," Soong murmured so only Ty-Sun could hear him.

"They are kept in seclusion then?" Ty-Sun asked, scarcely able to believe such a barbaric custom existed. Why would anyone wish to keep women separate? He smiled, thinking how indignant his concubines would be, particularly Spring Rain.

"That is correct, Your Majesty. Highborn women are never admitted to the company of men except for close male relatives, clergy, or privileged courtiers. The tsar's *terem* numbers nearly three hundred women. They live well," he added quickly, seeing the dismayed expressions on the faces of the two visitors. "They have Persian rugs, and tapestries, their religious books, their toilet articles, and there they paint or do their needlework, as well as tend to their prayers to keep them busy."

"But how will I choose among the Russlander women if they are kept secluded?"

"Ah, this is different, and so the women will be able to show themselves."

Ty-Sun nodded and noticed, not for the first time, that a number of the Russlanders were staring at him and Soong. Particularly noticeable were the Cossacks, whose expressions were closer to glares. The dwarf seated behind the tsar would dart frowning looks at Ty-Sun, who made an effort to avert his eyes.

"I don't think the Russlanders like us very much," Ty-Sun remarked as he cut into a chunk of venison. He was not accustomed to cutting his own meat, a service which was always performed by servants at home. Nevertheless, he did credibly well.

Soong nodded. "So I've noticed. Still, if the right woman is here . . ." He let his voice trail off and shrugged.

The feast tables were laden with hundreds of meats and delicacies, few of which Ty-Sun had ever tasted before, and Soong whispered that grapes had just been introduced into Russland.

Ty-Sun smiled, feeling superior to his host in that respect. He tried many different foods, but most he found particularly unpleasant, tasting too much of animal fat. The main course of meat was charred black on the outside, but blood ran when the meat was cut. Still, there were fruits that could not be spoiled, as well as many foods his own people had brought as gifts, and so Ty-Sun did not go hungry.

The evening's entertainment consisted of gaily dressed acrobats whose feats of tumbling and balancing were exceedingly rough and who rewarded each other with blows against the head. This produced guffaws of laughter from the tsar and other members of the court, and polite looks from Soong and Ty-Sun.

After the acrobats had rolled up their carpets and removed their other props, out came a burly man leading a great brown bear on a chain. The bear walked on all fours until the man jerked on the chain and the beast rose awkwardly to its hind feet. The trainer poked the animal, which managed to produce a growl that was far from threatening.

The tsar clapped enthusiastically, then nudged Ty-Sun and

grinned proudly. "Now, do you have anything like this in your Garden?"

"No, Your Majesty, we do not," the emperor replied tactfully as he thought of the graceful dancers with their fluid movements, of the women singers who plucked stringed instruments in accompaniment, of the poets who read their ballads that brought tears to his eyes with their haunting beauty, of the dazzling fireworks displayed on festival nights. No, the Land of Ten Thousand Willows had nothing like this.

The trainer cruelly pulled the chain again, its links clanking, and the bear lumbered about the stone floor, its stiff movements pantomiming human dance. The dwarf scampered out onto the floor to ape the animal's movements, and Russlanders roared their approval. Someone threw a chunk of meat at the beast, who grabbed the food in one immense paw and hungrily ate it. For the first time Ty-Sun noticed the bear's lean sides, its matted fur and the bare spots along its flanks.

He looked away.

Now that his attention had broken from the so-called entertainment, Ty-Sun realized that the back of his neck prickled, as if someone were watching him. As he raised his goblet to his lips, he glanced about casually, seeking the watcher. It could be any one—or more—of the hundreds in the dining hall, and yet . . . he glanced toward the darkness on the edge of the room. He felt as though something were there in the darkness, watching him and waiting. He swallowed the mead quickly, then turned back to his meal.

The dwarf returned to his stool, and the tsar hand-fed him with scraps from his own meal. The tsar kept stuffing the food in the other's mouth until the dwarf could scarcely keep up with his master. His cheeks were crammed with unchewed food, which he began spitting out. Meat juices dribbled down the creature's face, and he wiped his chin with the back of his sleeve.

Repulsed, Ty-Sun felt his stomach heave slightly, and he took a deep breath. It would not do to be ill at his host's table.

Course after course was served until Ty-Sun thought the servants would surely drop from exhaustion. As soon as a goblet became empty a servant jumped forward and filled it again with mead or ale, and as the hours of the evening progressed, the diners, as well as the entertainers, became more boisterous. Those not still eating were singing. Some of the Cossacks began dancing, rough tumbling sort of dances, and as they danced, they shouted and clapped, and encouraged their fellows to do more daring feats. They grabbed the dwarf and he danced with them, all the while keeping his eyes focused on Ty-Sun.

Finally, when he felt his head swimming with the unaccustomed strength of the mead, Ty-Sun excused himself, saying he was yet tired from his travels, and he and Soong left for their palace.

Tsar Mikhail had said before Ty-Sun departed that he would meet the first of the Russlander women upon the morrow, and as the emperor fell asleep that night, he wasn't certain that he wanted to.

10

The morning brought a break in the clouds which had hung low over Muscovy since the second day of their arrival, and a thundering headache to Ty-Sun upon awaking. He groaned, then closed his eyes again, but when the pain did not go away, he decided he would rise. He washed with the ice cold water left overnight in a ewer, then took a long walk in the palace gardens to clear his head. But not even that helped. Finally, he scooped up some snow and held a handful to his throbbing forehead, and after a few minutes, he felt some slight relief.

Much later in the morning, Soong and Fray Villadiego came out into the garden, and together the three men walked through the snowy streets of the Kremlin. Around Red Square was the tribune Lobnoe Mesto, or Place of the Brow, where the tsar delivered speeches. Also, many small chapels and churches, the tsar's zoo and public baths faced onto the Square. There were also a number of public taverns, and there they stopped to sample *kvas*, a mildly fermented beer made of black bread and various flavorings. Ty-Sun and Soong found they both liked it.

In the afternoon they returned to find a summons from Tsar Mikhail waiting in the person of Dmitri Raskonikov, so they left for the Terem Palace almost at once, with Ty-Sun stopping only to change into a robe of red silk with black dragons embroidered upon the back and the sleeves. Soong picked up the teakwood box with its precious contents of dragonleaves.

Mikhail greeted them warmly and asked how they had liked their tour of the Kremlin. Soong glanced at Ty-Sun, who replied that they had enjoyed it. Mikhail nodded sagely.

"Now, we will begin the presentation of those women who've arrived in Muscovy," Mikhail announced. "Most are highborn women, but not all, of course, and more will be coming into the city in the next few days, so there is no hurry for you to decide, Your Majesty."

"Thank you," Ty-Sun murmured, although it was his intention to hurry the process along as best he could. He glanced at Soong, who nodded his agreement. He was fast developing a dislike of this land.

Mikhail clapped his hands, with the malevolent dwarf doing the same, and the first of the women began to file in.

"They are the cream of our women," the tsar said, smiling broadly. "I think you will find nothing like them anywhere else."

Ty-Sun smiled after Soong had translated, then turned his attention to the women.

The women, all maids, wore open diadems with their hair plaited in a single long braid down their backs. Their gowns were like the robes of the tsar, full so that one could not see the outline of a body beneath the fabric. The gowns were red or gold or blue, and most were adorned with pearls. Each wore a necklace, a tiny golden cross hanging from it, around her neck.

And they painted themselves, too, unlike anything Ty-Sun had ever seen before. Some of the women had painted not only their faces, but their eyes, necks and hands—red, white, blue, black or other somber colors. When they smiled, he saw that their teeth were blackened—with preparations of mercury, Soong was told—because this was a sign of beauty. He dutifully relayed this to his emperor, who tried not to look aghast.

Yes, Ty-Sun knew he would find nothing like these women elsewhere. The ideal Russlander woman was not slim; in fact, the ideal was downright hefty, and while Ty-Sun might tend to some weight, he did not want it in his wife. Most of these women looked as if they could substitute as a plow animal, a thought which appalled him. Each one was very heavy, and the robes they wore did nothing to disguise that. Some had very pretty faces, some were close to beautiful, but he could only smile weakly when the tsar arched an inquiring eyebrow.

Ty-Sun indicated that Soong should open the box, and he selected a leaf and handed it to the first maiden, a dark-eyed blonde. She was pretty enough, but her rolls of chin repelled him. She looked at the leaf, then started to take a bite out of it.

Hastily Ty-Sun retrieved the leaf, asked Soong to thank her, and proceeded to the next one. She was slimmer than the others, and her brown eyes gazed boldly into his. He could have liked her as his empress, Ty-Sun thought, but when the minutes passed and nothing happened, he knew she wasn't the right one. He thanked her, and continued on to the next maiden.

Woman after woman failed the test, and for the first time Ty-Sun wondered if this had been the right way to determine his empress. Yet he saw no other choice. His bride had to be able to call to the dragons. Some of the Russlander women called aloud, but nothing happened. He sighed.

Hours passed, and still the line of maidens kept on. Mikhail ordered a halt for a meal, which Ty-Sun welcomed, and then two hours later, they were once more offering the leaves to the women. This continued with exhausting regularity until the evening was well advanced. Finally Ty-Sun begged Mikhail to halt the process for the day. The tsar did so, and Ty-Sun returned to his palace and promptly fell asleep.

The next day was the same. He saw blond women, and dark women, women with upslanted eyes that made him think of Spring Rain's, women with round, slightly popped eyes. He saw women with pretty smiles marred by the black teeth; he saw women that made him shudder.

All during this ordeal, he was aware of the dwarf staring at him, and this only served to make him more uncomfortable.

Finally, at the end of three days, Mikhail turned to him.

"Nothing?"

"I am sorry," Ty-Sun said in his most diplomatic of voices, "but none will do."

Soong translated. "None?" Mikhail demanded, completely astounded.

"None," Ty-Sun repeated.

"I will send for more," the tsar announced.

"Oh . . . thank you." Ty-Sun sighed deeply.

After they had dined, he and Soong began walking back to their palace. Along the way Ty-Sun shuddered. "They're all whey-faced, Soong, and built like water buffalo. I couldn't marry one of them, even if one could summon the dragons."

"I know," Soong replied gloomily. "I had thought to find better here. I think we should return to the coast in a day or so. Our time here is wasted."

The sound of slight scrambling came from behind them, and the two men whirled around, Ty-Sun's hand clasping the hilt of his sword. Standing not more than seven feet away was the tsar's dwarf. The creature grimaced at them, then turned and ran deftly down the street toward the Terem Palace.

"General Soong, you said that none of these people beyond Raskonikov understood our language?" Ty-Sun inquired casually.

"I said nothing of the sort."

"I see. Well, I think we can safely assume he understood us

perfectly. Perhaps we should return with all due haste to our quarters. I believe that our welcome at this court is about to end."

In the morning Ty-Sun was proven correct, for a politely worded note was sent to them, suggesting that they might wish to leave now because they were no longer welcome at the Muscovy court.

"Good, now we can get on with our traveling."

Ty-Sun sighed, then ordered the ministers to pack. When all were ready to leave, he stopped and turned to Soong.

"I'll be back in half an hour or so. Wait for me here."

"Where are you going?"

"Back to the Palace."

"Don't be foolish, Your Majesty. You aren't wanted there."

"I know that, but I have something I must do."

Soong shook his head and watched as Ty-Sun strode off through the snow toward Terem Palace. Yes, his emperor was definitely slimmer than when they landed at Archangel. He knew Ty-Sun disliked the Russlander food, and doubtless that helped. He smiled. He would see the emperor thin yet.

Soong waited for more than an hour and when Ty-Sun had not returned, he grew worried and started off in search of the emperor. But halfway to the palace, he was met with a startling sight. Ty-Sun was walking toward him, but he wasn't alone. At his side, minus chain or even a leather leash, ambled the brown bear they had seen "dance" at the feast in their honor. Ty-Sun was talking to the bear, and gesturing, and from time to time the animal raised its head to look at his companion, as if he understood the human's words.

Ty-Sun smiled as he stopped within a few feet of the general. "Close your mouth, Soong. You needn't look so astounded."

"What have you done?"

"I have bought this poor creature so that I might give him freedom. I didn't want him cruelly used."

Soong said nothing, contenting himself with thoughtfully stroking his moustache.

"Are you ready?"

"Yes, Your Majesty." Soong fell into step beside Ty-Sun and the bear, and when they reached the gates of the city, with the troikas following, Soong drew away that Ty-Sun might speak privately with the bear. Soong realized what he was thinking and snorted. Talking with animals, indeed! That would be the day.

The bear glanced at Ty-Sun, shambled a few steps toward the wilderness, then sat and watched over his shoulder as Ty-Sun got into the troika. Soong joined him, then glanced back. The bear had not run off as he'd expected. He gave the driver instructions to begin, and the man clucked to the horses. The sleigh slowly pulled away from Muscovy, and when Ty-Sun glanced back he saw a dark shape loping slowly after them.

"Stop!" Ty-Sun shouted, and without translation, the driver understood. He waited until the bear had caught up, then smiled over at Soong. "I think he wants to come with us."

"Well, you did save him." What was he saying? Soong demanded to himself. Did he believe the emperor's addled notion of talking to the bear? He must be getting daft in the head, too!

Ty-Sun spoke in a soothing undertone, then stroked the beast's head, and asked Soong to tell the driver to take a slower pace. Sighing, the general gave the man instructions, then settled back.

11

The return trip took far longer, due of course to the bear, who could not move as quickly as the troikas. Finally, when they arrived at Archangel, Spring Rain, who had watched for them each day, ran toward the sleighs. She stopped when she saw the great furry beast sprawled behind Ty-Sun's troika.

"You've brought back a bear, but no empress!" she exclaimed.

"Yes, my dear, and it's a very long tale, indeed," Ty-Sun said wearily. She saw that he had lost more weight, that there was more definition to his face now, and she helped him from the troika. As the couple walked toward *The Water Dragon*, the bear and Soong followed, and Ty-Sun explained how he had come to acquire the beast. Finally, when they reached the boarding plank, Spring Rain turned and gently touched the bear's scarred head.

"You poor thing," she said. "We'll feed you and take care of you now."

The bear made a deep rumbling in its throat, like a growl —only that it wasn't—as Spring Rain continued to stroke its head.

Soong sighed, seeing that the girl was lost to the animal's dubious charms as well. "Well, I suppose we ought to see about getting our new companion here aboard the ship."

Ty-Sun smiled wickedly. "*That* I shall leave in your capable hands, General." And with Spring Rain he walked up the plank to the ship's deck.

Soong and the bear eyed each other warily.

It didn't take him as long as he feared to coax the bear on board the ship, nor was it all that difficult, and once he had found an empty cabin for the animal, Soong reported to Ty-Sun.

Ty-Sun was staring at the tiny pool of pearls at the bottom of the crystal. Spring Rain sat in a corner of the cabin, her hands clasped in her lap.

"So many days lost," he said. "Gone now."

"Which is why we must be on our way as soon as we take on more supplies."

"You are correct, General. You are always correct." A sigh escaped Ty-Sun.

Soong glanced at him, then at Spring Rain, whose face was as worried as his own. Recently Ty-Sun had seemed less his old self than ever before. More and more he fell into dark reveries, and when Soong talked with him, he felt as though he were disturbing great thoughts with his trivial questions.

"My lord," Spring Rain said, going to him. "What is wrong?"

His eyes dark with sadness, he turned to her. "I've been unable to call forth the gods since we left the Willow Garden. This has never happened before. They've always come at my bidding—always. Why have they stopped now? Why won't they come when I need them the most? I could have saved all those who were lost."

"It wasn't your fault that those men died," she said softly.

"Oh, but it was. I am . . . was . . . their emperor, their Son of Heaven, and I failed them."

"You did what was only *humanly* possible, my lord. You acted quickly and saved many others from being lured overboard. It is true that some were lost, but that has always been the way of battle, and you must be glad that no more were killed." Ty-Sun said nothing. "I think, my lord, that the gods must not respond so far from the Willow Garden. It may be that they have little authority in this world."

"If the gods do not, who or what does? Does that mean there exist other gods . . . more powerful ones than those we have always known?" His eyebrows drew as he frowned. "Gods, such as that of Fray Villadiego, or perhaps some who are not as benevolent."

"I have watched him call upon his god many times, yet never has it appeared in our presence. Still, Fray Villadiego does not lose faith—particularly in himself. Is that not so?"

"Yes, Spring Rain, it's true." He beckoned to her, and she came to kneel before him. She relaxed then against him as he stroked her long hair.

"It seems to me, Your Majesty," Soong said, speaking for the first time, "that this has been the best thing that could happen to you. You're learning to do things on your own. No more depending upon the gods to get you out of some scrape. You must take the blame—or the credit—for what happens."

Ty-Sun frowned at this statement which was perilously close to treason. He glanced down at Spring Rain, who nodded her agreement with Soong, and Ty-Sun sighed. Was everyone against him today? He shook himself. He was too weary, and too discouraged, to think anymore on this matter. He would sleep, and in the morning, *The Water Dragon* and its companions would set sail for the lands south and west of Russland.

But that night and the following one Ty-Sun was disturbed by dreams in which an insidious voice whispered to him.

He couldn't make out the words, yet they disturbed him. The voice—whose was it, and why did it invade his sleep, his dreams? He had done no one any harm. Indeed, this journey was his first venture away from the confines of the Willow Garden and surely that could bring no injury to anyone.

On the second morning, he rose late, looking haggard, and was aware of the concern of Spring Rain and Soong. Even when he napped that afternoon, strange dreams interrupted his sleep. But he could never remember what the dreams were about.

He spoke little that day, and feeling more exhausted than he should, he went to bed early that night. But not long afterward, he awoke from a disquieting dream. He rose, and when one of his servants stirred, he told the fellow to go back to sleep. He pulled his robes about himself and stepped outside.

Overhead the sky was black, like the ink of an artist, and thousands of stars glimmered there. He thought he heard the high, fluting cry of a waterbird, but when he listened more intently he heard nothing but the soughing of the wind and the splash of water against the ship's hull. He could see the bright pinprick of light from the watch's fire on another ship.

The crisp air thrust into his lungs like icy daggers, yet it felt good because it helped clear his head. And he needed that.

He knew, as he had suspected all along, that they were being watched. The birds he'd seen . . . spies. And that unseen watcher whom he'd sensed in Tsar Mikhail's dining hall.

Watched . . . why? Because he was traveling outside the Garden? Because he was trying to find a bride? How could that threaten anyone?

A patch of darkness slid across the backdrop of stars, and automatically he took a step back. Whatever it was, it was gone in an instant, leaving the stars clear once more. He had to know, and there was only one way to find out who this watcher was. He went below to his cabin.

He returned then to the deck, knowing it would be best to

do this outside. In his hands he held the Orb of White Jade. It was cold as he stroked it gently. Taking a deep breath, he began spinning the Orb between his palms. With each spin it glowed whiter and warmer, until the Orb seemed to rise from his hands. Gradually his breathing slowed and his eyelids lowered as he fell into a deep trance.

Ty-Sun opened his eyes, expecting to find himself on the familiar silver-lighted astral plane, but instead he saw only blackness. A thick blackness that seemed to press against him, as if it were trying to smother him. Confused, he pushed out against it with his mind, felt it recede a little. Then he stared around, trying to get his bearings.

It was a plane of sorts, but not the one he customarily visited. Extremely flat as far as the eye could see, it had no distinguishing features at all. Nor could he determine what was the source for the dull sickly light that spread around him. There were no moons or stars overhead.

He took a few steps forward, hoping he might see something. The ground underfoot was hard, like solidly packed dirt, but it was cold, too, and the cold seeped through his shoes and up his legs, chilling and numbing him until he thought he would be barely able to move another step. And move he must, he knew, if he didn't want to freeze into position.

He walked for what seemed to be hours, but could not have been longer than minutes. Still he saw nothing. Was he the only one here? And where was this place? Surely he had come here for a reason.

Off in the distance, close to the horizon, Ty-Sun caught a flicker of movement, and he narrowed his eyes, trying to focus on what it was. But it was still too far away to see properly, and so cautiously he began walking toward the movement.

As he walked he remembered the Orb of White Jade and held it aloft. Wholesome light spread in front of him, and he saw finally what had caught his attention.

Long lines of hooded and robed men and women marched toward him. The lines were perfectly straight. No one straggled to the left or to the right. Everyone was in perfect step. Fascinated, he continued gazing at the silent men and women as they marched closer with every moment.

It was then that he began to note the details. All he could see of their facial features were orange eyes burning in skeletal faces. Their arms hung loosely in their sleeves, which came only to the wrists, and their hands were putrefying flesh, bloated maggots crawling through the scabrous fingers. Still, they made no sound, not from their mouths nor with their feet.

The hair prickled on the back of his neck, and he knew he shouldn't stand there any longer. He turned and hurried back in the direction he'd come, but when he thought he'd reached the right spot, he realized he had no way of telling.

And the hooded cadavers adjusted *their* direction, still heading toward him.

He broke into a run, not caring how it looked. So that he couldn't lose the Orb, he slipped it into a pocket. Behind him the ranks of marchers followed, never slowing down or speeding up.

When he was out of breath, he paused, and as he did so, the darkness above him parted, as though it had really only been clouds of gloom hanging in the sky. There was more light to see by now, but it was just as unhealthy as the gloom was before.

To his surprise he found something else upon the plane.

Not far away a crooked black spire loomed high into the air, almost to the rip in the clouds. It rose from the ground, as if it had been thrust roughly from far below the surface. Dead vines with hooked thorns, and rotting vegetation twisted about it. Droplets of moisture the color of blood trickled slowly down the spire's stone sides.

An unwholesome light flickered from the single narrow window set high in the spire. As he stared at the tower, Ty-Sun knew that within its dark walls he would find the unseen watcher. Knew that as well as he knew his own name.

He had come to find the watcher; now he had found the watcher. And he didn't know what to do next.

Yet he hadn't actually seen the watcher, had only seen the tower of the man . . . the woman . . . whatever it was. That wasn't quite the same.

He waited, not knowing what else to do.

After a few minutes, he took a deep breath, then coughed as the foulness of the air seeped into his lungs. He took a step forward. He would go to the tower, perhaps even into it, and he would confront that unknown watcher.

Without his knowing it, the ranks of silent figures had reached him, and now as he moved, they split smoothly, circling toward him.

Under his feet, the ground rippled, nearly tossing him off balance, then shuddered with some contained force. He spread his legs, trying to regain his balance, and another ripple spread through the plane. Only a few feet away, a fissure opened up, and noisome-smelling steam blasted upward.

The light in the tower had grown stronger.

Ty-Sun glanced at the silent figures, who made no move toward him, then at the tower, and he knew that he wasn't ready to face whatever was there. Not yet.

And so he turned and fled.

Immediately, the hooded figures rushed after him. Ty-Sun knew he had no chance of outrunning them, not when there were so many of them and so with a slight rasp of metal, he drew out his sword. The astral Dragon's Tongue gleamed white in the unnatural darkness, and as the first wraith reached him, he slashed at the creature. Dragon's Tongue sliced through the thing's trunk, and immediately it slumped to the ground, its robe now empty. Only a trickle of greenish ooze remained of the creature.

Feeling more than a little queasy, Ty-Sun took another deep breath and whirled to meet his next opponent. He slashed left and right, the still silent wraiths falling under the blade. No screams or cries of pain rose as he thrust the sword through their bodies. One hopped backward, out of range of Dragon's Tongue, and as Ty-Sun thrust the sword through one of its companions, the other creature jumped him from behind. Its long nails raked across his neck and back, and he slammed at it with the flat of his sword, trying to get it off his back where it clung like a leech.

Finally, the creature dropped off, and as Ty-Sun whirled, out of breath, blood dripping down the back of his robe, he saw that none of the creatures remained alive—or whatever they had been before he had used the sword.

He wanted a breeze to blow, to waft away the stench of the dead things tumbled at his feet, but no breeze blew. He coughed, then held his sleeve across the lower part of his face. When he turned to the tower, the window was black, and he knew the watcher stood there.

Shuddering, he began running. Suddenly a greyish root seemed to rise up from the ground before him and entwine itself about his ankle. It pulled, jerking him off his feet and as he fell, he slashed at it with Dragon's Tongue. He fell and fell, then screamed, and when he awoke on the deck of *The Water Dragon*, the Orb lay cold in his hands.

He returned below deck and carefully packed away the Orb, then sat on the bed. What had the vision meant? Who were those robed figures? Who was the watcher? Where was that plane?

Something itched slightly along his neck, and when he put his fingers there, a smear of blood came away on his hand. He shuddered and wiped the blood from his fingers, and for the rest of the night he did not sleep.

12

The next day, just after dawn had painted the sky pale gold and salmon, General Soong ordered the flotilla to continue southward. The ships had to go through a series of rivers and lakes and canals, which would take them to the Baltic Sea.

"Are you all right, Your Majesty?" Fray Villadiego asked as he walked along the deck.

Ty-Sun leaned against the railing, where he had stood for nearly an hour thinking of what had happened in his vision last night. A cool breeze ruffled his hair. At his side, Spring Rain did not greet the priest.

"Yes, fine. Why do you ask?"

"You look pale this morning."

"I didn't sleep much last night."

"Ah. Bad dreams?"

Ty-Sun glanced sideways at the priest, not sure if the Spaniard spoke sardonically. Yet the priest's face was innocent of any expression other than concern. He was imagining things, Ty-Sun told himself.

"Yes, a few uneasy dreams. Nothing to disturb me tonight, though."

"Let us pray not," the priest said softly.

Suddenly, the lookout on *The Water Dragon* cried out and pointed to something far above his head. Ty-Sun looked up in time to see the sky turning black with huge bird creatures, whose wings were red and yellow flames. Their eyes were dead black, their talons red-hot pincers. The birds shrieked as they swooped down and began attacking those on board the ships.

Without thinking, Ty-Sun called out to his gods, but when none came in the next moment, he grasped Dragon's Tongue, glanced at Soong, who'd pulled out his crossbow and was already loosing arrows at the firebirds, and began slashing at them as they darted toward him. One dropped to the deck at his feet, and Spring Rain leaped forward, thrusting a small dagger through the bird's neck. Immediately the flames were quenched, and only foul-smelling ash remained.

High above the hideous shrieks of the firebirds floated the cries of those being attacked. Out of the corner of an eye Ty-Sun saw some of his ministers cowering from the fiery talons. He shouted for them to get their weapons, but it was too late.

One of the junks—he thought it was *The Red Willow Dream*—was afire, its masts and sails burning brightly. With each scream he winced. On the ships, servants and courtiers kept busy, putting out the numerous fires being ignited on the deck.

"We're too heavily outnumbered," Soong cried. "Every time we kill one of these damned creatures, ten more fill the skies."

Ty-Sun nodded and stepped forward, slipping on the deck, now greasy from ashes and the blood of the injured and dead. Nearby Spring Rain slashed away with her dagger. In her other hand she held a small sword, which she wielded as if she'd been trained as a soldier. The heat from the firebirds grew with each passing moment. He was sweating heavily, his robes clinging to his skin, and in some places the silk was smouldering, as if any moment the material might burst into flames. He knew he must do something now. Soon—too soon—he and his people would be dead. He had come too far to give up now.

Commanding what strength he had left, Ty-Sun raised Dragon's Tongue high into the air, and red firelight gleamed on it. He forced all his concentration, his energy, into his words and focused on the sky.

"Storm Clouds, I bid you to come to us. Draw your energy forth and release it upon these hellish creatures. Come to us!"

A distant rumbling answered him, and overhead the white clouds that had earlier dotted the sky began turning black. The clouds oozed and roiled together, becoming a single solid mass in which jagged lightning flashed, and was answered immediately by thunder. Ty-Sun called out again, and the rumbling overhead deepened. Fat drops of rain started falling, and he raised his face to the rain, which washed the soot away.

Overhead the firebirds hissed, and as the drops of rain hit them, they sizzled and dissolved, falling into the sea as oily ash. As the water poured from the heavens, the last of the firebirds was destroyed, and the final fire was extinguished. Ty-Sun stared sadly at the fire-gutted junk, with its charred masts, and no survivors.

The unseen enemy had sent the firebirds to stop them, which meant that he was growing closer to his bride. Yet that gave him no feeling of triumph. Too much . . . too many lives . . . had been lost today.

Her face streaked with soot, Spring Rain took him by the hand and led him below deck.

"You must rest now. You have done much today," she said softly.

Exhausted beyond anything else, he nodded and allowed her to undress him, discarding the charred robes. She bathed his face and hands with water scented of cinnamon, then put clean robes upon him, and even before his head touched the pillow, he was asleep.

For a long moment she gazed down at him. In the past few weeks he had lost so much weight that she almost didn't recognize him. Gone was the roly-poly emperor, replaced with a leaner-faced stranger. A grim-faced stranger. She touched the tight lines formed between his eyebrows and they eased a little. She rose and left him to sleep.

On deck she found General Soong supervising the terrible chore of cleanup. She said nothing as she watched the dead prepared in white mourning clothes for burial at sea. She was very numb and tired from the battle with the firebirds, and she had lost many friends today. Afterward, she turned to the general.

"We lost more today than last time."

He nodded. "Each attack grows worse, and I anticipate more of them as we go on. Whoever—whatever—sends these creatures is determined to stop the emperor before he can find his bride."

"I do not think this person will succeed, General Soong. My lord is far too strong."

"I hope so—for all our sakes." Taking the girl's hand, he led her away from the scene of death.

When the junks docked along the coast of the Dominion of the Teutonic Order, messengers were waiting. These had visited the nearby kingdoms of Sweden, Prussia and Poland; Ty-Sun's request had been turned down, albeit politely. At the next stop, messengers reported that women had been tested in Lithuania, but none had proved acceptable. The Papal States, Republic of Venice and Kingdom of Naples had expressed disinterest in allying themselves with a "pagan" emperor. Women in the Holy Roman Empire were tested with the dragonleaf. Emperor Ferdinand II allowed this because he was always interested in the possible acquisition of more land. Unfortunately, none of the women had been the right one. Too, the messenger had barely escaped with his life. The Holy

Roman Empire was in the midst of a religious war, which seemed to be spreading throughout Europe.

Failure. All failure, Ty-Sun thought as he paced about the deck. Everywhere he turned every court refused him. Where would he go next? What countries were left? Time, after all, was fast running out. He glanced at the crystal, at the growing pile of pearls.

Soong suggested they try France, home of the Bourbon King, Louis XIII. Ty-Sun agreed. After all, what choice did he have? They docked along the coast and made their way to Paris.

Louis, a Roman Catholic, suspicious of the Easterners, was reluctant to meet with them until at last Fray Villadiego intervened. Louis was suspicious of the priest as well, for the Jesuit was Spanish, but at least they were of the same religion. For some time he spoke with the king, and finally Louis agreed to meet with Ty-Sun.

Dressed in his most radiant robes, Ty-Sun carefully explained his mission in seeking a bride, with Villadiego acting as translator for both monarchs.

Louis raised an exquisitely arched eyebrow. He had been eying Ty-Sun and Soong as if he had seen nothing like them before, and in all probability he hadn't. "You seek a wife from the French?"

Ty-Sun bowed his head ceremoniously. "If the gods deem it so."

"Gods? What gods?" Louis looked impatiently to the priest for explanation.

"It is simply an expression among his people," the priest replied smoothly.

"I see." Louis fell into a deep study, and minutes passed as he said nothing.

Ty-Sun felt uncomfortable. This audience chamber was grand with its high ceilings decorated with painted panels, carved mouldings, and beautifully woven tapestries. Everywhere he glanced, too, he saw gilt, and while he thanked the gods there was much less red than there had been at Tsar Mikhail's palace, he found he didn't care much for the court, much less the monarch. That, of course, he told himself firmly, didn't mean he wouldn't—or couldn't—find a bride here. He glanced at the Jesuit, who made a slight motion with his hand, as if to say, *just wait, be patient*.

Ty-Sun could be a patient man, but not now, especially since General Soong was constantly reminding him of the urgency of his search. Even at that moment Soong chose to clear his throat, then looked meaningfully at the emperor.

"Your Royal Highness," Ty-Sun began.

"I have considered," Louis said, as if he hadn't heard the other man's words.

Villadiego hurriedly translated.

"Yes?"

"I have decided that you may stay here and conduct your search."

Ty-Sun inclined his head. "You are most gracious, Your Royal Highness."

"Yes, I am." Louis smiled, dismissing all of them from his supreme presence.

After that, the French king proved a fairly affable host, wining and dining the entourage from the Willow Garden, providing them with many hours of entertainment. Yet whenever Ty-Sun inquired when he might meet with the French ladies, Louis would wave a negligent hand.

"And just what does that mean?" Soong demanded, once they were out of the king's chambers.

"It means, I think, that for some reason he's delaying us," Ty-Sun replied slowly. "We've been here for over two weeks, and I've seen only a handful of French ladies, those I've met at the court. Although I must admit, they are quite exquisite." He had never seen such low-cut bodices on a woman before, nor any woman or man dressed as elaborately as these French noblewomen. It amused him that they stared at him as much and as intently as he stared at them.

Soong stroked his moustache furiously. "Hmm, I think you're right, Your Majesty. It does seem that the king could gather these women much more speedily—France is a very advanced country, after all. Yet every time you press him, he replies that France is a large nation. Russland was big, too, but Tsar Mikhail acted quickly. Hmmm, this bears looking into."

"Soong."

"Yes?"

"What if I have somehow overlooked the woman who is to be my empress? What if she was in some village in Russland and never received the news to come to Muscovy? What if the woman was in one of these countries that refused to receive me? What if I never meet her?" His expression was troubled.

"I don't think that's happened."

"But, what if it has?"

"If it has, then we'll probably never know, Your Majesty."

"You mean we'll just continue this . . . this futile practice."

"Yes."

Ty-Sun shook his head. "Then why do we bother with it?"

Soong's eyes glittered fiercely. "Because we don't know any of that for a fact, Your Majesty. Because you might meet the woman here, or in some other country we have yet to travel to. France isn't the last nation on Earth, you know."

"It feels like it," Ty-Sun muttered.

"What was that?"

"I said I'll talk with Fray Villadiego, and see what he can do to hurry things along."

"Good."

Ty-Sun had started to leave, but Soong's voice stopped him.

"Your Majesty."

"Yes?"

"It's about Villadiego."

"Yes?"

Without expression, Ty-Sun stared at him, but Soong sensed that the emperor was in no mood to hear what he wanted to say. It could wait until another day; would have to, now.

Soong bowed and sighed. "I am sorry, Your Majesty, but the thought has completely fled from my old mind. These days my brain is like a many-mended net—it lets escape more fish than it captures."

Ty-Sun smiled. "Very well, old friend."

Soong watched the emperor leave, and wondered just how much help the Jesuit priest truly would be.

Fray Villadiego must have been put to some good use, because the very next day Louis announced that at the end of the week, he would be presenting the French women at court.

Ty-Sun met this announcement with his usual good humor, now restored, and with much relief. Winter was drawing to a close already, and soon . . . too soon . . . it would be spring . . . and he would be that much closer to the end of his three years.

When week's end came, he stood by Louis's side, as one by one the French noblewomen were presented to him. They were altogether prettier and much slimmer than the Russlander women, and did not indulge in that horrible practice of blackening their teeth.

General Soong, looking very handsome in silk robes of green and gold, opened the teakwood case and presented each woman with a leaf. From time to time Louis would glance hopefully at Ty-Sun, but the emperor would sadly shake his head. Each time Ty-Sun would hold his breath, waiting for that moment, but each time nothing happened. What if they hadn't devised the proper test? Doubts assailed him, draining him of his confidence, of his hope. He felt watched at this court, too, and as he scanned the crowds of courtiers and their ladies, he wondered which of them was the spy.

Many of the French women thought the leaves quite attractive, and flirting with the general, tried to take one as a memento. Soong, seemingly oblivious to their charms, managed to hang on to the leaves.

At the end of a long, exhausting evening, interspersed with much good wine and wonderful sweets (in which Ty-Sun found himself overindulging), finally, when he had reviewed what seemed to be thousands of French women, he sat back in his chair and closed his eyes. He was no closer to finding a bride. He could feel the exhaustion threatening to overwhelm him, but he fought it, kept it under control. This was just what his enemy wanted. Once he acknowledged his exhaustion, defeat would soon follow, and the enemy would have what he wanted.

Ty-Sun thanked the king for his patience, even though secretly he believed that Louis hadn't done all that much, and within a few days they returned to the French coast and their ships.

"Where next, Soong?"

Soong unrolled a map and spread it out on the table, weighing the corners down with several mugs.

"We are here, Your Majesty, at the coast of France and across here," he moved his finger westward from France, "is the island kingdom of Britain, a land long known for its magic."

"That might prove interesting." He didn't sound convinced.

"I think so."

"Magic, you say?"

"Many different forms exist there, and it is said that Britain is one of the oldest lands in the world. Far older than even the Willow Garden."

"That's impossible."

Soong spread his hands. "It's what they say."

"Well, do you think I should go there?"

"If Your Majesty would like to."

"Soong."

"It is the country closest to us now."

"Oh very well," he said, his voice peevish, "set sail there, if you must."

"Very well, Your Majesty." Soong tried to restrain his smile of triumph. "With Your Majesty's leave, I will inform the captain of our course."

Ty-Sun inclined his head. Once Soong left, the emperor glanced at Fray Villadiego, who had spoken little that evening.

"Have you nothing to say, Fray? What of a game of chess?"

"If you so desire, Your Majesty." As he set up the gameboard and arranged the pieces, the priest glanced up at the emperor. "Are you so sure that you should go to this Britain?"

"What?" Ty-Sun, studying his lines of chessmen, looked up, slightly startled. "What do you mean?"

"As the good general said, it has much magic in it, but not always the best kind. Too, it is a strict country, as far as religion is concerned. The English are not at all tolerant."

Ty-Sun said nothing.

"I hope that you will not be disappointed." He watched as the emperor opened the game by moving his bishop's pawn.

"Where would you go, if you were making suggestions?" Ty-Sun inquired casually. He watched as the priest's opposing pawn swept forward two spaces.

"I would go to Spain—but then I am partial to that sunny country, hailing from it as I do. And there is also Portugal, a land long renowned for its explorers, something which I know is dear to Your Majesty's heart." Ty-Sun smiled. "And there are the countries of the Mediterranean. The Barbary Coast is a good choice, as are many others. Perhaps the smaller countries would afford a better opportunity, Your Majesty."

"Perhaps. Aha! I have captured your bishop!" He whisked the white piece off the board.

"But I have put your king in jeopardy," the Jesuit said with a slight smile. "Check."

"Oh, bother," Ty-Sun said, and forced his mind back to his game.

13

Ty-Sun awoke late that night from a pleasant sleep without dreams to find his comfortable bed pitching wildly about under him. He staggered to his feet, bumped his head on an overhead beam, cursed softly, then groped in the darkness until he found his robe. He pulled it on, then buckled Dragon's Tongue at his side. He rarely left without it anymore. From on deck he heard the sounds of shouting.

He found Soong already on deck, while *The Water Dragon*'s crew fought to keep the junk upright. Gale-force winds whipped the fragile sails about, and loose lines dangled from the masts. Like a huge silver coin, the moon rode high above them, but the light was only intermittent because of the black clouds that scudded across the moon's face.

"What's happening?" Ty-Sun shouted. He stared about at the wreckage on the slippery deck. A great howl rose from below deck, and the bear stuck its nose outside hesitantly, then disappeared just as quickly as the boat shifted and the animal lost its balance.

"A squall, Your Majesty. Came up out of nowhere. Here, tie yourself to this lead—this way you won't wash overboard."

Ty-Sun took the rope from the general and cinched it around his waist, making sure the knot could not slip loose. If he needed out of the rope quickly, he would simply cut it with his sword.

"But I don't understand. When I went to bed the sky was clear, the water calm."

"I know. I suspect this storm highly—there's nothing natural about it. Watch out!" He jumped forward, pushing Ty-Sun away. Part of a mast splintered and crashed down, landing where the emperor had stood just a moment before.

Ty-Sun nodded, silently thanking the general. "What about the other ships?"

"*The Jade Butterfly* and *The Partridge Sky* have both capsized."

"And those on board?"

Soong shook his head sadly. "All gone, every last one of them."

Ty-Sun lowered his head in sadness. On *The Jade Butterfly*

had been his actors and musicians. Gone now. Like those on *The Partridge Sky*, like those in the Great Ice and those who died because of the firebirds. Three ships lost now, and so many aboard them dead.

Too many.

You are to blame, a small voice deep within him whispered, and he raised a hand as if he could brush away the doubts. To blame . . . your folly, your conceit . . . these caused those deaths.

"No!"

"What?" Soong shouted.

"Let me see what I can do," he said, but Soong merely nodded and was already turning away to help the sailors save one of the spars.

The Water Dragon rocked violently, knocking Ty-Sun off his feet and to the deck, now resting at a steep angle, and as he slid toward the railing, he was caught by the rope tied around his waist. The rope tightened, keeping him from going overboard, and when the ship finally righted itself, he slowly got to his feet.

The wind screamed past his ears, and overhead thunder boomed. Not the thunder of his making, not a friendly force this. Somewhere in the darkness he heard the crack of wood breaking apart, and beyond that a high barking, a deep rumbling.

Ty-Sun raised Dragon's Tongue and called out. The silver light of the moon slid down the length of the sword, entering his body, welling within him, giving him power. He raised his hand and in the darkness it seemed to glow with its own light.

In his mind's eye he imagined the ships and saw the unnatural force that blew them, that tossed them like toys upon the increasingly rough waters. He knew this was the handiwork of his enemy. The Enemy. In that otherworldly scene he positioned himself leeward of *The Water Dragon* and *pushed* with all his strength to keep it and its sister ships upright. The force slammed violently against him, pricked his mind and his body, and although he wanted to cry out in pain, he kept thrusting at the junk, keeping it upright. Only dimly was he aware of the others, and once he thought he heard a woman's scream.

Spring Rain was hurt; he must go to her. The absolute control in his mind wavered momentarily, and instantly he knew it was a trick of the Enemy. Spring Rain was all right.

Darkness passed into day as the storm continued, unabated.

The wind had shredded his clothing, whipped his hair across his eyes until he thought he was blind, scraped at his skin, leaving his cheeks and hands raw. Bone-deep weariness threatened to overwhelm him, yet he couldn't let go. He knew if he gave in and stopped now, the storm . . . the Enemy . . . would win.

The rays of sunlight that somehow squeezed their way through the ragged storm clouds glimmered along the sharp edges of Dragon's Tongue, strengthening him. If only the light would hold out. If only he would.

At times he was aware of Soong at his side, talking to him, but the words meant nothing. Once Spring Rain was there, and he knew she sponged his grimy face with scented water. He knew thirst and hunger, and physical discomfort, and pain, but still he had to keep standing, keep pushing. He had to beat back the force that opposed him.

In his mind a tiny dot of blackness appeared, and as it rolled toward him, it grew, becoming a roiling void that surged forward, threatening to take him. Screaming, he thrust Dragon's Tongue into it. Sparks flew from the sword, piercing the darkness, and with each cut of the weapon, the void lessened until nothing was left. He stepped forward, swinging the great sword about as the wind dwindled and the clouds lightened.

He sagged to his knees, and would have pitched facedown on the deck if Soong hadn't been there, as he had been for most of the four days of Ty-Sun's battle with the storm.

"It's all right now, boy," Soong said gruffly, and for a moment Ty-Sun thought he was a child again and had just fallen from his pony for the first time. He had lain in the dirt, his knee skinned, and he had wavered between laughing and tears. Finally, Soong who had been instructing him, had come over and gently helped him to his feet and said it was all right, all right, all—

Ty-Sun blinked, and saw that it was day. The sky was blue, without clouds, and the sun was shining, while a brisk wind blew.

Spring Rain knelt by him and handed him a cup filled with water. He drank greedily, not caring that it spilled down his chest, onto his hands. She gave him cup after cup; he swallowed each mouthful as if he had been in the desert without water for a week. She wiped away the sweat and grime that marked his face, and began tending the wounds left by the wind.

"Don't drink too fast, boy," Soong said. "We don't want you foundering like a pony."

Nodding, he forced himself to slow down, then wiped the remnants of his sleeve across his face. His eyes felt gritty and as he looked around, he saw the damage caused by the storm. The main spar on his ship still stood, but the others were gone, and debris, as well as bodies, lay scattered across the deck.

A sharp pain thrust through him, like the cut of a sword. More deaths upon his hands. He looked down into the cup of water and in the reflection he saw the black spire. He looked to Soong.

"Who . . . what . . . else?" His words were croaked, his throat rough.

"We lost *The Moth* last night."

Weariness surged through Ty-Sun. There were only three ships left now, out of seven. All those people, dozens . . . hundreds . . . for whom he had been responsible. Whom he had failed. Dead, all dead. In his head he heard mocking laughter.

Because of him, a voice within him whispered, all because he'd insisted on bringing a large entourage, specifically against Soong's advice. Because he'd been too foolish to realize that what his general said was true. He had needed his silly comforts . . . page boys, musicians, grooms, cooks, his own tutor. And now they were gone, dead, far away from the peacefulness of the Willow Garden. Because of him. He put his head in his hands and would have wept, but no tears came.

"You must rest," Spring Rain said. "Come lie down now."

He nodded, too tired to disagree. He closed his eyes, but all he saw were the faces of the dead.

"Do you need help below?"

"I'll manage."

Ty-Sun took a step forward and nearly fell over. Spring Rain leaped to his side to steady him, and he smiled down at her. She looked weary, too, and he wondered what she had done during the four days. Had she slept at all? Had any of them? He saw the sailors, silent and sober-faced, as they went about repairing the junk. They were watching him. After all, he was their emperor. He was Ty-Sun. Gently he pushed aside her hands and stood straight, throwing back his shoulders. He would go below on his own, without any assistance.

He walked slowly toward the hatch, and when he had reached the first step, a cry sounded from above. Ty-Sun looked up at the watch. Spring Rain and Soong turned as one and saw what had brought the watch's cry.

Sails upon the horizon. Heading toward them. The sails of pirates.

No, no more, Ty-Sun wanted to cry out. The words formed on his lips, but no sound came.

"Break out the arms!" Soong called.

With the sails half-down, *The Water Dragon* was unable to escape, and all too quickly the two pirate ships were upon them. Cannon boomed out, and in horror Ty-Sun watched as the balls ripped great yawning holes in the sides of *The Hummingbird*. The vessel began taking on water, and within minutes she was sinking.

With a savage cry he leaped forward, Dragon's Tongue raised. Sparks of sunlight flew from the metal, and he aimed it at the first pirate ship. The pirates swarmed along the deck, preparing to board the stricken vessels, but just as they were preparing the grappling hooks, fire erupted on their ship. They screamed as it crept toward them, engulfing them in a shower of sparks.

The battle raged for hours, and Ty-Sun drew upon his final reserves of power and strength. He had little left, enough perhaps to withstand this onslaught by the Enemy. But, after that . . .

Finally, with two of the pirates' vessels burning, the other turned tail and fled, and those on the two remaining Willow Garden ships cheered.

"The danger . . . gone, black spires . . . ," Ty-Sun mumbled, and then he collapsed.

Spring Rain and Soong took him below deck. Just that morning she'd had the few remaining servants straighten the disorder left over from the storm. Ty-Sun's bed had been made fresh, and there they carefully laid the unconscious man. Spring Rain pulled a sheet up over him and stared down at him.

"He's grown so thin these past few weeks."

"He's become a man," Soong said. "He's lost weight, but he won't miss it. He's changed since we left the Willow Garden, and I'm pleased with what he's become. I knew it was always there, waiting to be called forth. He's hardened, too, grown far stronger, and that's good. This isn't a game of chess that he plays."

For a few minutes longer they watched him, then Soong spoke again.

"I think it's obvious that Britain is the right choice, Spring Rain. Look at the resistance we've met since we made the decision to go there. Yes, I look forward to reaching that island."

"I pray that my lord will be strong enough to meet the challenge of the Darkness that lies ahead," she said, and bent down to kiss Ty-Sun's cheek.

Her eyes had been downcast as she spoke, and not for the first time did Soong wonder what lay within her mind. Did she truly want Ty-Sun to marry? After all, at present she was the most important of his concubines. But after his wedding, she would become little more than a companion of past years.

Still, he knew she was loyal, and that she loved Ty-Sun with all her heart. She would help him however she could. He'd seen that these past days when other women—and men—might have cowered below deck in terror; instead Spring Rain had been constantly at Ty-Sun's side attending him, or coming to Soong to see what she could do. As far as he could see, the girl knew no fear, and, not for the first time, he wished that she had not been born a peasant.

He turned away from her and as he stared down at the emperor, Soong realized he shared her hope, too. Ty-Sun had grown stronger. But was he strong enough? Only time would answer that question.

PART II

1633

14

Martin Bleeker, manservant to the gentleman Robert Thadwell, Lord Elphinstone, paused to savor the moment. It was already half past six on a crisp foggy March morning, and he could smell spring in the air for the first time. Indeed, he could.

Though it was early in the day, he was already running errands for his lordship, and although this well-traveled street took him along the bank of the River Thames and was quicker than any other route, he didn't normally take this way. It was here that slaughterhouses maintained their killing pens, where sewage from the city's ditches sluiced into the river, where warehouses produced rat-infested filth.

Today, though, the current flowed swiftly, carrying away any unnatural elements dumped into the waters so that the Thames looked and smelled more like the great river it had been only half a century ago, when it had been a broad expanse of pure water.

Martin could see the brown of cattails clinging to the sharp sides of the banks, and close to the opposite bank several white swans glided through the waters. Here and there on those trees whose long branches dipped down toward the water, buds were forming, heralding the approach of spring. Coots with their silly black and white faces danced across the surface of the river. An otter, its long whiskers twitching, a fish in its mouth, loped along the bank, no more than a few feet away from the boy, then slid, belly-down into the water.

Not quite twenty yet, Martin had been given by his impoverished parents into service in Lord Elphinstone's bustling household when he had just turned six. Though greatly protested by him at first, it had proved a fairly wise decision by his mother and father, who shortly thereafter died of a fever, along with his eight brothers and sisters.

Once acquainted with the ways of the Thadwell household, he had started as a page boy for his lordship and his lady, (now sadly deceased through the auspices of the smallpox outbreak some years before) and having proven a diligent and intelligent worker, he had risen through the ranks of the household staff until now he was one of Thadwell's most trusted servants.

He delivered his master's private messages, not only to his lordship's friends, political and otherwise which he had aplenty, but to Lord Elphinstone's current mistress, a pretty girl several years younger than Martin himself. He was on his way there with an important message to her when he paused to enjoy the morning air. Lord Elphinstone would trust no one but Martin with these errands, the boy thought proudly.

He wasn't very tall, was Martin, but he was muscular and fairly slim. He was always running from one place to another for his master, and rarely had time to eat, although sometimes the cook, a tenderhearted woman, would pack him a lunch of ham and cheese to take along on his errands. His stomach had been grumbling for the past half an hour, and he wanted to stop and eat the bit of food cook had packed, but he knew he should wait. At least for another half an hour.

Martin had a square, honest face with wide cheekbones, large blue eyes fringed with dark curling lashes, a nose slightly on the large side, and shoulder-length hair the color of brown autumn leaves that curled slightly on the edges, no matter how often the boy tugged at it. His hands were square, too, the fingers blunt-tipped, but long and capable.

Lord Elphinstone often remarked that his young servant had the hands of a true craftsman, but Martin thought his lordship was teasing, something his lordship did quite often. It was hard at times to tell if his lordship was serious or not.

He wore good buff breeches, heavy leather shoes meticulously polished each day, and a hand-me-down white shirt of his master's, its cuffs slightly soiled already. He wore a coat, too, the blue of service, and gold braid had been sewn across the lapels and the cuffs and pocket flaps. Martin was very proud of the braid; it signified that he had some standing of import in the Elphinstone household.

Silky tendrils of mist rose from the Thames, obscuring most of the river. The mist drifted upward, then slowly curled toward the banks. The air was chilly still, and he shivered just a bit. Soon, though, the sun would burn off the mist and warm him, although by that time he hoped he would be at Mistress Marsh's house. Doubtless she would reward him with a cup of warm cider, as she had done upon other occasions.

For the moment, though, he squinted through the mist watching the numerous boats as they plied their way up and down the river, and listening to the calls of the boat and bargemen. Suddenly a great outcry rose from the boatmen, and startled, Martin turned his head in the direction of the sound.

At first he didn't see anything, and he wondered what all the fuss was about, but then quite suddenly, and without warning, something large and dark loomed through the whiteness. Martin squinted, the better to see what it was. It looked remarkably like the prow of a ship, although if it were, the prow was nothing like any he had ever seen in all his years. Slowly and silently the craft glided through the mist, and he got his first good look at it.

The vessel was huge, but wide and low, and its hull was painted gold so that it glistened in the sunlight. The square sails were red and gold, the fittings all brass, and on the prow was carved a strange beast, its mouth opened in a ferocious roar. A dragon, that's what it is, Martin told himself.

A second ship, almost identical to the other except that it was a little smaller, followed the first from the fog. Its figurehead was an impressive bird, the likes of which Martin had never seen before, either.

He stared at the deck of the first ship, where a tall man stood. He had long black hair and wore a magnificent red and black garment that trailed as he strode about. His expression was stern, almost fierce; his hand rested on the hilt of a huge sword. And what looked like an immense brown bear sat at his side.

Martin rubbed his eyes, but the bear was still there and was looking about him with what seemed like fairly human interest. A much smaller and older man with snow-white hair and a flowing moustache, dressed in leather armor, leaned against the far railing and scowled. He seemed to be talking to himself. Standing a few feet away was a third man, dressed in a black cassock. A priest, Martin thought, and wondered what a priest was doing with these odd folk.

A fourth person took Martin's notice, too. A young woman, tiny and fragile-looking, with ebony hair that swept below her hips. She wore an odd-looking gown of pale blue, and Martin, who could only gaze at her, thought her the most beautiful woman he had ever seen. Certainly she was prettier than Lord Elphinstone's mistress who was quite a looker, all right. At that moment she glanced his way, and Martin felt as though he were melting.

He took a step closer to the bank so that he might better see. He had forgotten the outlandish boats, the tall man, even the bear. He had to see the woman much closer.

The tall man spotted Martin watching and hailed him in precise, if somewhat stilted, English.

"Good day, Englishman." Here he gave a slight bow. "Go tell your king that Ty-Sun, Emperor of the Land of Ten Thousand Willows, has come to meet with him. I will wait here."

Martin's mouth dropped open. He was astounded. What was this man talking about?

"Go on, boy, run now to your king." The tall man smiled.

Martin shrugged, then turning, he set off and ran all the way to the palace without stopping once to gasp for air. He only hoped he'd see the young woman when he returned.

"Well, now you've done it," Soong grumbled as he watched the boy disappear into the distance. "That boy's gone and run off scared witless. You should have let me handle it." He glared at the young emperor, as if he could be trusted to do nothing right.

"Nonsense, General," Ty-Sun replied frostily. "I know perfectly well what I am doing. That boy is obeying my bidding and has simply gone to inform his monarch of my desire for a meeting."

"You hope."

"I *know.*"

"Gentlemen, gentlemen," said Fray Villadiego easily. He smiled.

Soong glared at the priest. After the storm and subsequent attack by pirates, the two remaining vessels had put into a French port for repairs. Those had taken far longer than Soong had anticipated, and with each passing day he chafed at the delay. He knew though, too, that no one aboard *The Water Dragon* or *The Phoenix* was prepared to sail yet, and so they had rested and taken on fresh stores, and in that time Soong had begun teaching English to Ty-Sun. The latter was fairly good at learning new languages, but the lessons had not gone well.

Ty-Sun, who seemed to recover quickly from his exhausting ordeal, had continually complained about the illogic of the language's construction, as well as its spelling, while both Soong and Fray Villadiego, who spoke English fluently, explained that this was simply the way the language had developed. Ty-Sun threw up his hands in disgust, but was finally persuaded by Spring Rain to sit and learn. She had sat with them, too, so that she also might learn English, and Soong had been grateful for her presence because it quieted Ty-Sun.

A small barge sailed by, and the English sailors stared. Soong's scowl deepened.

Minutes passed, and the sun rose higher in the sky. The fog was fast burning off. The bear yawned wide, showing his long teeth, then lay down to take a nap. Soong glared at him.

"Now what?" Soong demanded when still more minutes had elapsed and the boy hadn't returned. People were gathering on the riverbanks and gaping at them. Soong supposed these Londoners had probably never seen anything like the two junks.

Ty-Sun spared his general an imperial glance. "Now, we wait for a messenger from the king—or perhaps even the king to arrive himself."

"I wouldn't hold my breath on that—I don't think the king will come. The English aren't ones to bow and scrape before others."

"He should. He should be impressed that the emperor of the Land of Ten Thousand Willows has graced his uncouth land with his presence."

Where was the reasonable emperor of the past month? It was as if by resting, Ty-Sun had regained all the conceit and bad temper he'd had back home. Soong sighed to himself.

"I'm sure he doesn't see it that way, Your Majesty. In fact, I'm quite sure he won't even have heard of the Garden."

"Barbarian," Ty-Sun said genially, and raised his hand to wave at a ship of grinning Englishmen as it passed *The Water Dragon*.

"Indeed," Soong said neutrally, and they settled down to wait.

15

"What's this now? Some strange boat—boats—are sailing up the Thames?" the guardsman demanded. Thomas Spiggott was a big man—not from foot to head, but rather from side to side, and his clothes, in the blue and gold of the royal household, ill-fitted him and looked as though he had long outgrown them. His face was round and slightly on the red side with a long nose and protuberant eyes, and when he talked, his breath reeked of sour ale. He stood at the entrance of Hotspur, the Stuarts' favorite residence in London, and in the way of Martin Bleeker who knew he had to see the king.

"Yessir." Martin nodded vigorously.

"Tell me again what you saw."

Once more the young man patiently repeated how he had stopped along the riverbank while on an errand, and how only moments later he had spotted the remarkable craft, and the man who had spoken to him.

Spiggott scratched his head. "Here now, I've never heard of no Ty-Sun, boy, much less no Land of Ten Hundred Willows."

"Ten Thousand Willows," Martin corrected, not for the first time.

"Sounds fairly outlandish to me," the fellow grumbled, scratching his side. He belched, then wiped his mouth on his sleeve.

"It is, sir," Martin admitted, "but in an interesting manner. The ships were really quite beautiful, unlike anything I've ever seen before." He would never forget that first glimpse of the dragon boat as it silently glided out of the fog.

"Could be those Spaniards up to some devilish trick like in Good Bess's time."

Martin shook his head slowly. "I don't think so, sir. Those on board the ship didn't look Spanish at all. And there was a woman, too. A very beautiful one," he said wistfully.

Spiggott threw him a sharp glance. "A woman, eh? Not many women allowed on ships. Bad luck, you know, boy. Well, lemme see. It must be the Frenchies then." Martin shook his head again. "Who're we fighting this year? Who aren't we fighting?" The guard paused to scratch his side again, then spat off to the right. "Must have been those Catholics."

Martin was a member of the Catholic faith, but held no enmity toward anyone, no matter what their religion. His master was even more tolerant, with a household of Catholic and Protestant servants, as well as several Jews to oversee his business concerns. There was no one quite like Lord Elphinstone, Martin thought proudly. "No. I think they came from farther away than even Italy."

Looking astonished, the guard belched again. Martin tried hard not to make a face. "Farther away than Italy? What's beyond that ungodly place, boy? That's where all them Popish sorts be rioting about one thing or the other, isn't it?"

"A fabulous place lies far to the east," Martin said, his voice slightly awed. "I heard about it when I was in school."

"School. Pshaw." Tom Spiggott spat again and Martin jumped quickly back to keep from being splashed. "No one learns anything there."

"I learned about Cathay."

"What the hell is that?"

"A fabled land where dragons and beautiful birds and unicorns live and the mountains are made of rubies and sapphires, and it rains pearls. 'Tis a truly wondrous place."

"Hmmph. Sounds like a pack of nonsense to me, boy. Somebody been filling your head."

"I know what it sounds like, but it isn't. Not really." His voice took on a pleading note. "Will you let me through? I should tell the king. After all that man—another king, too—talked to *me*. He asked me to get word to the king, and you wouldn't want him not to know."

"Well, don't know if I should, but you look honest enough, boy. I'll send word, but in the meantime you wait here."

At the end of an hour Martin still waited outside Hotspur Palace. Some time ago his initial enthusiasm had waned. He had succumbed to utter boredom, and now sat to one side of the door, his head propped in his hands. For the entire hour Tom Spiggott talked about his experiences in the army twenty years ago, which Martin found even more boring, and which he suspected were made-up, anyway.

As Martin waited he grew more and more unhappy. In the midst of all this, he'd neglected to deliver Lord Elphinstone's rather urgent message, and while his master was the most even-tempered of men—most times—he did have a rare temper which he would unleash upon occasion. And Martin feared this would be one such occasion. He'd probably lose his job. He'd be out on the streets by morning. By nightfall at the latest, he told himself glumly. Why'd he have to pause and enjoy the morning? Why couldn't he have just gone about doing his duty, doing what was expected of him? Even when he was a small child, his father said that his dreamy nature would get him into trouble, and it looked like he was right.

And even worse he would never see the beautiful woman again, because doubtless if someone did believe him and come out of the Palace, and if he could lead them back to the Thames, the fabulous boats and their occupants would be gone by now, and everyone would accuse him of dreaming. And doubtless they'd clap him into jail, because there was probably a law against what he had done, although he wasn't sure what he could have done wrong. He lowered his head miserably. Whatever was he going to do?

Suddenly he raised his head, looked around without seeing, then jumped to his feet.

Spiggott broke off in the middle of yet another military anecdote. "Here now, boy, what's nippin' at yer balls."

"I can't wait any longer, but send this message as well. Ask His Majesty to look out the Palace windows at the Thames in half an hour. Will you tell him that? Will you, please, sir?"

The guard's voice was rough, but he nodded. "I'll send a message along."

"Please."

There was something about the boy's earnestness that softened the guard. "Very well, boy, I'll see what I can do. Half an hour, you say?"

"Yes. Now, I must go." With that the boy ran off without a backward glance.

The guard shook his head slowly, then stepped inside the entrance to insure that the boy's message was carried to the king. After all, he'd given the boy his word, and by Christ, he'd keep it. The boy was a damned fine listener, and perhaps the lad would come back, and he could finish his story about his deeds in His Majesty's army.

Martin raced back to the spot along the river where he'd first seen the boats, and by the time he saw that they were still there, he was out of breath. His heart hammered, and his head felt as if it were about to explode. He bent over, resting his hands on his knees, and drew in great gasping breaths. When he could stand upright again, he vigorously waved his arms and yelled, "Hallo! Hallo, aboard the gold craft!"

There was some movement on board as one of the soldiers noticed him and then went below momentarily. Only seconds later the tall regal man in the magnificent robes appeared on deck.

"Yes?"

"I'll take you to the king!" Martin yelled.

"Where is he?" Ty-Sun asked.

Martin pointed. "Up the river, sir, just a little further from here. You'll see his palace. He'll be there."

"Very well. Lead on, Englishman."

Grinning, Martin nodded and began trotting up river and into the heart of London.

16

Charles Stuart, absolute ruler of England, glanced up from his papers, wishing for an interruption. He was the only surviving son of James I, the Scottish monarch, who had succeeded to the English throne upon the death of Elizabeth I, and Anne, the daughter of Frederick II of Denmark.

Charles was a slim, faintly handsome man, of very short stature, who'd begun life quite ill and consequently was unable to walk until the rather advanced age of seven. As he grew older, he counteracted this physical weakness by becoming athletic, but his frailty proved not to be his only disability.

Until he reached the age of ten, he spoke with difficulty. Few people understood what he said, and as he grew older, he stammered. He lessened this painful trait by speaking slowly. It was also something his enemies used to point out as proof of the slowness of his wits. Meticulous in his dress and manners, unlike his father, who had revolted everyone by his grossness, he was a collector of fine paintings and books. His light brown hair was long and curling, and he wore a thin moustache and a pointed beard.

In a nation now sharply divided in its religious preferences, Charles was a Protestant king of the Anglican faith. Within the past one hundred years England had undergone a complete religious turnabout several times over, with resulting mayhem. Henry VIII split from the Church of Rome, and in doing so dissolved and looted the numerous Roman Catholic monasteries for their immense wealth. He also actively persecuted those clinging to their original faith.

No sooner had England seemed to recover from this ordeal than it was ruled by a Catholic monarch in the rigid and overly zealous person of Henry's eldest daughter, Mary. She promptly set about restoring Catholics and in turn persecuting the Anglicans. In the reign that followed, that of Henry's second daughter Elizabeth, the Church of England was restored, Roman Catholicism virtually outlawed, and a new Protestant sect known as Puritans burgeoned in power.

It was all exceedingly confusing, even to someone as staunch a Protestant as Charles. Basically he was a good man who wanted to serve his country, but he was caught between these three forces, and to further add to the turmoil, he'd married a French woman.

France was a Catholic nation and the traditional enemy of England. Henrietta Maria, daughter of the late French King Henry IV, and sister to the present French King Louis XIII, was a fervent Catholic. She added her own pressure by continually urging her husband to leave the English Catholics alone.

To make matters worse, there were those in Parliament who felt that the monarch should no longer rule absolutely. These men were allied with the Puritans. Charles's side supported the divine right of monarchy with less interference by Parliament.

Each side plucked at him, trying to push him one way or the other, and from day to day Charles wondered just what would happen. Today was no different than countless others since he'd succeeded to the throne. Members of the various religious groups were present, hoping to discuss with him their fears and hopes. Their fears were always of the other religion, and their hope was that he would completely outlaw any other sects.

He sighed. Why ever had he sent that messenger away? The man had told some outlandish story about a boy outside the Palace, saying some foreign king in a boat wished to see him. Charles had dismissed him without comment, but now he regretted it because it might have proved diverting.

Charles returned his attention to the man named Cromwell, who was talking once more.

"The laws are far too lenient, as you well know, Your Majesty, and they must be strengthened immediately." Oliver Cromwell was a short, heavyset man with a swollen and reddish face, brooding dark eyes and brown hair chopped off at his ears, in the fashion favored by the Puritans. He was a member of the gentry, and of Parliament. His brows were dark and pulled together in what seemed a perpetual frown, and Charles had rarely seen him smile. He also had a sharp voice, which the king could pick out above all others.

"Which laws are those?" drawled Robert Thadwell, Lord Elphinstone.

Cromwell shot him a scowl, which only served to strengthen Elphinstone's smile. "You know which laws I refer to, my lord."

"Ah, the ones for—or rather, against—the Catholics, a repressed minority, I believe." He continued before Cromwell could speak. "It is an interesting historical note, you know,

Mr. Cromwell, that not even a century ago, 'twas the Puritans who stood in the very same spot now as the poor Catholics."

"You allege that because of your own miserable religion."

"Come, Cromwell, 'tis no need to be so offensive, although I sometimes think you cannot help it. Your religion is merely an offshoot of the Anglican, which in turn derived from Catholicism. And as we all know, the Christian religion—as well as the Moslem—owes its beginning to the Jewish faith." All the courtiers in the room turned to stare at him, recognizing his words as heresy. His smile deepened. "Which means, that although the Puritans might deny it with their hearts, they are nonetheless related to the Catholics."

Elphinstone smiled amiably. He stood slightly taller than Cromwell, and had somewhat plain but comfortable features. His brown eyes always seemed to look sadly out of his thin face, no matter how often he smiled or laughed. His hair flowed to his wide shoulders, and he wore a long, curled lovelock. His moustache and small beard were neatly trimmed.

While Cromwell was attired in somber clothing, Lord Elphinstone appeared dressed like a peacock. His deep lace collar was the most intricate design, while his trunk hose, that came to just below the knees, and his long coat were of green satin, the sleeves embroidered with gilt thread. Elaborate diamond roses glittered on his shoes, and he'd tucked a lace handkerchief into one side of his belt. A large plume decorated his wide-brimmed hat. Few of Charles's courtiers dressed as well as Elphinstone or spent as much money on finery.

Cromwell's face darkened as he took a threatening step forward.

"Gentlemen, please," Charles said somewhat weakly, "there will be no fighting in my chamber. Pray remember where you are."

Cromwell nodded, while Elphinstone merely grinned and bowed mockingly.

Charles wasn't sure how far the two men would go—whether blows would be exchanged. That sort of thing had happened many times before in Parliament, where tempers heated beyond the point of endurance and good manners. Was there nothing, he wondered, more volatile than the discussion of religion?

"It is well known that the Catholics have sold their souls to the Devil to obtain great power. Many openly practice witchcraft and murder innocent babes to obtain blood for their foul ceremonies."

Elphinstone opened his enameled snuffbox with a click that interrupted Cromwell. He smiled graciously, offered the box to Cromwell, who gave him a disdainful look. Elphinstone took a pinch of snuff between his thumb and forefinger and regarded it momentarily.

"You have proof that the Catholics are in league with the Devil, Mr. Cromwell?"

"I have certain papers."

"Papers can be forged." Elphinstone finished his snuff, slipped the box back into his pocket and proceeded to use his handkerchief.

"These are sworn affidavits."

"Sworn, no doubt, before Puritan magistrates, after the testifiers were persuaded ever so gently by Puritan lawmen."

Cromwell's face turned an ugly red, and Charles feared he would burst a blood vessel.

"Come, come, now, gentlemen. I will tell you what I think." The King indicated the papers spread before him. "I have read the various arguments tendered, and my feelings are much the same. Mr. Cromwell, I cannot continue persecuting the Catholics who—" What he would have said next, they never knew, because at that moment a second messenger, slightly out of breath, burst into the room.

"Your Majesty," the man said, bowing low, "gentlemen, I am sorry to interrupt."

"You'd best have a good reason," Cromwell said, glowering even more. He gave Elphinstone a dark glance, as if this all might be his fault.

"Your Majesty, I have come in haste to beg you to look out your window at the river."

Charles blinked, sorely perplexed. Was this some new scheme to gain attention by one of the groups? Yet what could it accomplish? Look out his window, indeed! At the river? Why, he had seen the Thames many times.

"Please, Your Majesty, the young boy at the front door, desires that you look outside. He seems very earnest."

"A boy? I don't understand." He looked to Cromwell and Elphinstone, as if they could explain what this meant. "Who is he?"

"He says his name is Martin Bleeker."

"Good God!" Lord Elphinstone exclaimed.

Charles glanced at him for an explanation of his outburst.

"Martin is one of my servants, and a boy to be trusted. But I can't imagine how he comes to play a part in this."

"Your Majesty—" Cromwell began.

Charles stroked his thin moustache. It wouldn't hurt to look out the window, and indeed, he did need to stand and stretch, perhaps even take a walk along the balcony for fresh air. Spring would soon be here, for which he was heartily glad. And there was far too much hot air in this room.

"Very well." He pushed back his chair and stood, feeling the soreness of his muscles ease somewhat. He went to the French windows in his office, then paused as one of the liveried servants sprang forward to open them so that the king could pass through them.

The messenger quickly followed behind the king with Cromwell, Elphinstone, and several curious courtiers bringing up the rear. Charles stepped out onto the balcony, which nearly hung over the river, as the palace was built along the bank. A story below him the Thames flowed quickly, with the sun now almost overhead. He leaned his hands against the railing, then glanced over at the silent messenger.

"Well?"

"The boy said half an hour, Your Majesty, and it is nearly that time."

"Very well."

Charles looked upriver, and saw nothing remarkable beyond the usual swans, then glanced downstream. What was he to see upon the Thames? What wonder—or horror—would there be? And of whose making?

Suddenly he straightened, and took a step forward until his legs pressed against the stone barrier. What in God's name was that?

"Look, Your Majesty!" the messenger cried, pointing. "Look!"

But Charles needed no prompting. He stared in absolute amazement as the immense boat with a dragon on its prow, and its smaller companion, sailed into full view of Hotspur Palace.

17

"Good God, what is it?" His Majesty exclaimed as he stared at the strange sight that sailed on the Thames opposite the palace.

" 'I saw two ships come sailing by,' " Elphinstone sang lightly, " 'Come sailing by, come sailing by, I saw two ships come sailing by'—no, it doesn't ring right. Three is a much better number, after all. What do you say, Mr. Cromwell?"

The Puritan ignored him. "Foreign ships, by their looks, Your Majesty."

"Indeed, Mr. Cromwell," Charles murmured. Foreign ships, the like of which he'd never seen before. He glanced at the messenger for explanation, but received nothing more than a puzzled look. Clearly he hadn't expected this, either.

"What can they be?" the messenger asked.

No one answered immediately, then Cromwell stirred slightly.

" 'Tis a Catholic plot," he muttered.

"Good God," Elphinstone replied, "not again. Why, no doubt you would take the thundering in your chamberpot to be a Catholic plot as well."

This time Cromwell did step closer, intending to hit Elphinstone, but his arm stayed, then dropped to his side, as his attention was caught by the larger of the ships pushing closer to shore.

Charles and his courtiers stared at a black-haired man on board the ship. His colorful garb was outlandish, like a woman's dress in a way, and yet totally unlike it. His features were unusual, with uptilted eyes, and a face like a hawk's. His bearing, though, was every inch as regal as Charles's. Beside him stood an older man wearing a fierce expression, and to the other side sat a rather large brown bear.

The tall man raised his hand in silent greeting.

"A demon," Cromwell said, pushing away from the railing slightly as if he believed that being too close was dangerous.

Charles waited for the other to do something, but then wondered if he should respond first. But how? Nothing like this had ever happened to him—or his father—or anyone in his family. Could this dark man be a demon? He didn't look much like one, but then Charles had never seen a demon, or an angel, before. Was this some sort of divine visitation?

"I believe he's calling to you, Your Majesty," Elphinstone said.

"Greetings, Your Majesty," the man on the ship called. He was glancing with curiosity from one face to another on the balcony, apparently uncertain just who was king of England.

"He speaks English," Charles observed aloud, rather unnecessarily.

"Yes, Your Majesty."

"Hello," the man called again.

"What shall I do?" Charles asked in an undertone to the others.

"I suggest greeting him, Your Majesty."

"An excellent idea, Lord Elphinstone." What incredible clothing the tall man wore! Were those dragons embroidered upon his robes? *And* a dragon upon the ship's prow, too! "Hello, there! Greetings to you." He paused, then blinked. "Who are you?"

"My name is Ty-Sun, and I am emperor of the Land of Ten Thousand Willows."

Charles and Elphinstone exchanged glances, while the latter shrugged. He had never heard of the place, but that didn't mean it didn't exist. Elphinstone coughed genteelly into his handkerchief. "Excuse me . . . Your Highness, is it? Yes, good well, Your Highness, where is this Willow Land?"

"Far to the east, beyond India," the short, white-haired man replied. The bear growled.

"Perhaps they're from Cathay or Japan, Your Majesty," Elphinstone said. "Certainly I don't believe he's a Russlander, even as outrageous as they are. Generally, they look rather like Europeans, while these men most certainly do not."

Charles continued staring down at the man staring up at him.

"Why are you here?" Elphinstone called, since no one else on the balcony was coming around to that pertinent question.

"I have traveled many thousands of *li* to meet the illustrious Charles Stuart, king of England. He is one of you?"

The English king preened slightly at the compliment. "I am he."

"I am very pleased to meet you, Your Highness," Ty-Sun said with a bow.

"And I you . . . Your Majesty." Was that really how one addressed an emperor? he wondered. He would have to have that investigated.

For the last few minutes the other balconies along that side of the palace had been filling with various courtiers, ladies-in-waiting, and assorted servants who had noticed that something unusual was happening. Their conversation buzzed like flies on a drowsy summer's afternoon.

Charles glanced at Cromwell. He was suspiciously quiet, and he wondered what the sly fox was up to. Someone stirred to his right and he glanced over to see Henrietta Maria by his side.

"You mustn't keep the man waiting down there, my dear," she said. "You must invite him into the palace." The queen's English, marked by an accent, which, while soft, only served to remind her subjects of her origins—and religion. She was a tiny woman, almost child-size, with an animated manner, and lively black eyes.

"Yes, yes, you're right, my dear. I will invite him into the palace."

"Do not see him, Your Majesty," Cromwell said, taking a step closer to the king. " 'Tis obvious he's a man of no account, and not who he pretends to be. It might be a plot to somehow harm you."

"Harm me? Whatever for?"

Cromwell shrugged. "You do have enemies, Your Majesty, not only in this country."

"You needn't remind me of that," Charles replied somewhat peevishly.

"Do whatever Your Majesty wishes to," Elphinstone said amiably as he took out his snuffbox again. "It might be very interesting."

"I just don't know." He glanced at Cromwell, then at Elphinstone, then at his wife.

"Charles, please do have him come to the palace," Henrietta Maria pleaded, her plump hand resting on his arm. "Please see this man at once."

Thoughtfully Charles stared at the ship and its unusual occupants. He was reluctant to make a decision, because he suspected that no matter what he decided, his entire life would be different from that moment on.

In the end, it was the gentle-spoken Henrietta Maria who prevailed, as she had done more than once upon other occasions, and Charles agreed to meet with Ty-Sun a few hours hence.

Eventually the balconies emptied of the numerous palace occupants who stared curiously at the strange ships and even stranger people in their river. Even the boy whoo Ty-Sun had first hailed had left the dock to go inside at the bidding of his master. Eventually Ty-Sun's own sailors and people stopped staring around at the palace, and Soong ordered he ships docked so that they all could get down to business.

"What was your first impression of the English king?" Soong asked as they went below the deck. Spring Rain followed with the bear at her heels. She had been fearful of it at first, but it followed her everywhere now like an immense lap dog.

"I wasn't sure which one was king. I rather thought it was the tall man in green."

"So did I." Soong threw himself into a chair and stroked his moustache. "I wasn't highly impressed with Charles Stuart. He was somewhat indecisive. For a while, I thought he would turn us away."

"My fear, too, although he does seem friendly enough. But let us remember not to make any stray remarks within hearing of dwarves or such, eh, Soong?"

The general chuckled. "No, not this time, I think, my friend."

"Come, Spring Rain, let us change our robes so that we may charm the hearts of these English."

She smiled, while the bear rose to its full height and roared.

"Your Majesty," Ty-Sun said when he was ushered into Charles's resplendent chambers. He thought this palace much more tasteful than that of Tsar Mikhail's, and less artificial than the French one. He particularly admired the large paintings hanging on every wall. A small entourage of General Soong, Spring Rain, Fray Villadiego, and a handful of others had accompanied him in his progress from the docked junk to Hotspur, but only Soong had gone in with him to see the king.

The others remained waiting in an antechamber.

"Your Majesty." Charles had hastily consulted his ministers of protocol as soon as the audience had been arranged, and these gentlemen, all of impeccable manners, averred that they'd never known such a situation to arise before, and thought perhaps an Eastern emperor might be addressed as "Your Majesty," as would a king, although of course to be considered far less on a royal scale.

"Your Highness." Ty-Sun bowed to Henrietta Maria, who smiled at him. He also nodded to the other English gentlemen who stood in the room. He recognized the one in the green whom he'd first thought was king. He did not see the dour man anywhere.

"I must admit that I was quite . . . er, amazed . . . by the sight of your ships sailing up the Thames. Rather remarkable, don't you think so, my dear?" He raised an eyebrow as he looked at his wife.

"Indeed, love. I've never seen anything like it, nor read of it, either." Clasping the arms of her throne, she leaned forward ever so slightly. Ty-Sun could not but notice that the bodice of her silvery gown was rather more low-cut than he was accustomed to seeing, and that the roundness of her breasts forced above the tight line of the satin reminded him remarkably of ripe peaches. Certainly Russland had offered nothing like this with its heavily bundled women. "Why is it that you have come to visit us, Your Majesty? Beyond meeting my illustrious husband, that is."

"Ah," Ty-Sun said, forcing his eyes away from the pleasant sight of the queenly bosom, "you see, I have come on a mission."

"A mission," Charles said, nodding sagely as if he already understood what Ty-Sun meant. God forbid, was the man some sort of religious missionary? He forced a smile. "Er, what sort of mission?"

Ty-Sun's expression was extremely grave. "It is one of a personal nature, Your Majesty. I am searching for a bride."

"A bride! How delightful!" Henrietta Maria cried, her black eyes sparkling. "And you have come all the way to England in your search?"

Charles looked stunned, as if this reply were the last thing he would have expected.

"Indeed, but I think I must first explain. Within the last

year, upon the death of my father, I have become the emperor of the Land of Ten Thousand Willows. That is a land that lies far to the east."

"Cathay," Charles muttered.

"Indeed, the Willow Garden is only one part of Cathay, as it is called in the West. As emperor, I am guardian of the dragons of the earth, who have over the past centuries fled to my land for protection. However, a prophecy was made upon the occasion of my birth that if I did not marry within three years after the death of my father, the dragons would disappear for all time, and indeed the very safety and existence of the Willow Garden and Earth would be threatened, too."

"Oh dear!" the queen exclaimed. "That would be a terrible thing."

"Yes," Ty-Sun replied gravely.

Charles looked extremely skeptical. "And you have come here to England looking for a bride. Did you try elsewhere?"

"Yes, Your Majesty. We have gone to other countries and I have sent messengers, but no bride has been found. I have an additional problem, beyond simply finding a suitable woman. You see, there is only one way of determining the right bride, and that is done with something called the dragonleaf."

At that moment Soong stepped forward and opened the box he carried under his arm. The scarlet and gold herb gleamed upon a cushion of black velvet. The Stuarts leaned forward to better see it. Elphinstone, who had been silent thus far, stepped forward, and as he gazed down at the marvelous herb, he felt the power radiating from it. He glanced up to see Charles staring at him, and he gave a barely perceptible nod. Yes, he believed what the emperor was saying.

"This is the dragonleaf. The dragons feed upon it as a delicacy, and when my true bride touches it, she will be able to call to the dragons, and they will come and surround her."

"What a beautiful story," the queen said.

"It is more than a story, Your Majesty," Soong said gravely, speaking for the first time since the audience had begun, "it is the only way our land—and the whole of Earth—can survive."

"Yes, yes, I see that." The king drummed his fingers upon the ornately carved arm of his throne. "And you want to travel throughout England and test each woman you find,

Your Majesty? Won't that take too long? You said you had been traveling for some months now. Aren't you running out of time yet?"

"No, no, Charles," his wife said. " 'twould be far better for us to organize a ball here and ask all the ladies of the land to attend."

"Oh, I see!"

"Yes, I think a ball held here would be an excellent idea," Ty-Sun said. "It would give us enough time to rest—we have met with many obstacles coming here—and would allow the women time to arrive."

"And if your bride is not among the fair crop of English women, what then?"

Ty-Sun exchanged looks with Soong. It was something he had never wanted to consider, yet he knew he must. "If that should happen, Your Majesty, I think that all is lost."

18

Spring Rain's eyes met Ty-Sun's anxiously as he and General Soong left the audience chamber. She slipped up to him, putting a delicate hand on his arm.

"Well, my lord, did all go well?"

He smiled down at her. "Yes, my dear, it did. The king and queen have graciously proposed to give a ball in my honor next month. That is sufficient time for us to rest, and for invitations to go out, and then for attendees to reach London."

"That is good to hear, my lord," she murmured, although her eyes were downcast.

"Excellent, Your Majesty," Fray Villadiego replied, with what sounded to Ty-Sun like false heartiness. But perhaps, Ty-Sun told himself, he was simply tired and hearing things that didn't exist. "Next month, you say?"

"Yes,Father. I know that we are running out of time"—here he glanced to Soong—"but Their Majesties insisted that a proper ball could not be given any time before that. And so a month it must be."

"Will we stay upon the ships, or will we be given rooms in the palace?"

Ty-Sun smiled at the priest. "In the palace, for which I am heartily glad. I am tired of beds that rise and fall with the tides!"

"Ah, here come the king and queen now," Soong said, clearing his throat softly.

Charles and his wife had left the audience chamber and were now approaching the cluster of visitors standing in the hall. Behind them strolled the man in green, who was smiling amiably.

Ty-Sun bowed in their direction, while the two English monarchs gazed at the other members of Ty-Sun's entourage. Henrietta Maria smiled when she saw the Jesuit priest, then she saw Spring Rain.

"Is this your . . .," she paused, her brow knit. She had been about to say "wife," although of course, this young girl couldn't be the emperor's wife. *That* was the reason he was in England. He was too young to have a daughter this age. A sister, perhaps? Such a pretty girl, and so very tiny, too, even smaller than she, and with the thinnest eyebrows she had ever seen. Did she pluck them, or had they grown that way? "Is this your sister, Your Majesty?"

"No," he replied smoothly, unaware of Soong's rising eyebrows, "Spring Rain is my favorite concubine." He smiled at the young girl, then gently touched one of her cheeks.

Henrietta Maria's eyelashes fluttered slightly. "Concubine?" She glanced at her husband for an explanation, but being just as perplexed as she, he was unable to do anything but shrug.

"I think, Your Majesty," said the man in green as he stepped forward and introduced himself as Lord Elphinstone, "that the term the emperor uses is not the one with which we're familiar. I believe that it signifies an important member of the imperial household, the equivalent of a trusted advisor."

"Oh, I see." She relaxed visibly.

Soong gave a curt nod of approval to the man. The Englishman might look like a peacock, but he had a sharp brain. He should have warned Ty-Sun that the Europeans did not approve of concubines. Kings might have any number of mistresses and the resulting bastards, but a concubine was something altogether different. More respectable, by the Garden's standards.

"And this is your priest? You are Roman Catholic, Your Majesty?" Queen Henrietta Maria asked happily, obviously hoping to find one of her own among these odd foreigners.

"No, Your Majesty," Ty-Sun replied politely. He thought he understood what had just occurred, but thought he'd best consult with Soong later. He wished to step on few toes in his stay in London. "This is Fray Villadiego, who came along some months ago to the Willow Garden as a missionary."

"And have you been successful, Father?" the queen asked.

"Alas, no, madame, for the good citizens of the Willow Garden are firm within their religion."

"I am sorry to hear that, but we shall have discussions of our religion and theirs sometime, Father. That topic is a particular favorite of mine, and perhaps if you would not mind and if His Majesty could spare you, you might lead me in my prayers some morning." She flashed a warm smile at him.

"I would be honored, Your Majesty." He made a courtly bow.

"Villadiego? Is that not a Spanish name?" Charles asked suddenly, as if he was having trouble keeping up with the conversation.

"Yes, Your Majesty." Villadiego's smile remained even, but as he glanced at Elphinstone his eyes flickered slightly.

"Well, come, my dear, we must leave our guests to rest. Ah, first they must be escorted to their rooms." Charles glanced about somewhat blankly, as though looking for someone.

At once Elphinstone stepped forward to his monarch's rescue. "I will escort them, Your Majesty, if you only will permit me."

"Of course, of course, my boy."

Elphinstone smiled. He was nearly the same age as the king, who was but three and thirty.

The English monarchs lingered for a few more minutes, chatting of inconsequential matters, then swept off toward another part of the palace for some prior engagement they had to honor. Elphinstone turned to the small party and bowed to each one in turn.

"This way, please."

As they walked toward the other end of the great antechamber, Spring Rain noticed that they were being discreetly followed by the boy whom Ty-Sun had hailed that morning. Occasionally he would stop and pretend to study a painting hanging in front of him.

"One of my servants, Martin Bleeker," Elphinstone explained when she mentioned this. A slight smile touched his lips as he beckoned to the boy. "Martin, come here, please."

"Yes, Lord Elphinstone." He rushed over and stopped, slightly out of breath.

Elphinstone smoothly made the introductions and was amused to see Martin turn beet-red when introduced to Spring Rain.

"Pleased to meet you, mistress . . . ma'am," the youth stammered, then looked away. Had he a cloth cap in his hands, his master thought sardonically, he would have been twisting it.

"Would you care to help me, Martin?"

"Help you, my lord?"

"Yes, I am escorting these good people to their suites, and perhaps you can help me in pointing out the sights along the way."

"Oh, yes, I'd like that, sir, if you would only allow me!"

Ty-Sun and Soong exchanged amused looks, while Elphinstone only looked skyward.

"Did I not ask you, lad?"

"Oh, sir, you did, indeed. Thank you, sir!" He fell in with them, or rather alongside of Spring Rain, and from time to time he would sneak sidelong glances at the young girl.

Ty-Sun did not pay much attention to the brief tour that Lord Elphinstone conducted on the way to their quarters. He was much too tired to think of anything but a real bed, a bed that did not move. The Englishman promised them a more complete tour of the palace when they were sufficiently rested.

He led them up a magnificent set of stairs, carved of solid walnut, their guide claimed, and at last, they reached their rooms. Elphinstone said he hoped they would be comfortable enough and said that they would have servants available at any time, and to use the bellpulls in each room if they desired anything. Once more he bowed, then clapped Martin on the back.

"Let's go, boy."

"Oh . . . oh yes, sir!" Martin gave a shy smile at Spring Rain, who smiled in return.

Once they were outside in the corridor, Martin danced away from his master and turned around, his eyes shining with excitement.

"Did you see that, my Lord? She smiled at me. At me!"

"Indeed, I did." He chuckled at Martin's look of astonishment. "Well, lad, you are a handsome boy, after all. You will turn the head of more than one woman in your life, I think."

"But she smiled at me."

Elphinstone sighed slightly. "Yes, indeed, she did, lad." It really didn't matter what he said, he didn't think the boy heard anything.

They walked some time in silence, then Martin glanced at his master.

"I overheard you talking with the queen, my lord. What does 'concubine' mean?"

Oh Lord, Elphinstone thought, how do I explain it without breaking his heart?

Ty-Sun looked around. The room in which he found himself was immense. Ornamentation of white vines and pomegranates, animals and birds decorated the plaster ceiling some twenty feet above his head. The walls were all painted, with elaborate scenes stretching from a halfway mark of wood to the ceiling. Ornately carved wooden furniture, some of it covered with rich cloth, was clustered here and there in the room, and along one wall was centered a massive marble fireplace with doors on either side. He found this room very impressive.

Opposite the fireplace was yet another door, leading no doubt to more rooms, as did the other two. Light gleamed off the polished wooden floors, and he stepped across to the arched windows. The windows were all closed, with a result that the room was stuffy. He ordered them opened, and breathed deeply as a breeze filled with the scent of the river wafted in. He leaned his elbows on the windowsills and gazed out. Good, he could see the river and his two remaining ships.

Farther down the river, he could see the immense structure they had passed as they sailed up the Thames. The Tower, Fray Villadiego had called the fortress, and Ty-Sun had been distressed to see the human heads thrust upon pikes there. With a small cry Spring Rain had turned away.

He shook his head. He was tired and needed to rest soon before he collapsed. He glanced around at Soong who had just returned from inspecting the other rooms.

"Well?"

"They are excellent. Far better than what we had in Muscovy." Soong pointed to the doors by the fireplace. "They might lead to sitting rooms, and a rather large dining hall. I don't know who they think will be here with us, but it might be useful. Through this door are more rooms, bedrooms and such. I have found one that I think would be good for you to use. It looks secure, and as always I will position a guard at the door."

Ty-Sun smiled. Soong was always thinking of his security, for which he was eternally grateful. He nodded, and let Soong guide him to the room he'd selected. This one was much smaller than the first, and thus more intimate, and Ty-Sun approved. A cheering fire had been built in the fireplace, this one of speckled marble, and he crossed over to it and held his hands out. The furnishings here were just as grand as in the other rooms he'd seen, yet warmer, more personal. Draperies of maroon velvet hung across the windows, dimming the light that entered the room.

A handful of his remaining servants were already unpacking

some of the few pieces of baggage that hadn't been lost in the storm. He heaved a great sigh as he considered the lost men and ships. Would that never leave his mind?

Soong glanced at him. "You look terrible. You should lie down."

"I plan to."

"Here now," Soong called, clapping his hands at the servants, "this can be finished later."

They all bowed and left the two men alone. Ty-Sun, who felt as though he was swaying slightly, sat down in a chair covered in rose and silver material. His fingers traced a pattern of tiny flowers along the arm.

"What do you think, Soong?"

Soong stroked his moustache, then clasped his hands behind his back. "Too early to tell, at least today, Your Majesty. I'm tired, too, and should rest. We'll be able to consider all of this when we're rested."

"Their Highnesses seemed very polite, very congenial, although not all that astute. Still, that is only my first impression of them. I liked them far more than Tsar Mikhail."

Soong chuckled. "This is a much more refined court than the one at Muscovy. I wonder what they will think of your bear."

"I don't know, but I suspect I should leave him on the ship, although it might be amusing to lead him about London on a leash." Momentarily his eyelids, feeling extremely heavy all of a sudden, dropped, and when he opened them, he saw Spring Rain kneeling before him. The room was darker than before, and he looked around for the general, but didn't see him.

"Where's Soong?"

"He left when you fell asleep."

"Oh." He had thought he'd just closed his eyes for a moment; he'd no notion he had actually fallen asleep. He yawned, then smiled at her.

"I will help you to bed, my lord."

He nodded, feeling suddenly that words were quite beyond him. She helped him to his feet, and he was pleased to find he could still maneuver fairly well. At least, he didn't fall down.

A large bed was pushed along one wall, and he started to sit down on it, until Spring Rain indicated she wanted him to continue standing. He did so, while she pulled his robes off. Then she thrust back the covers, thick and warm-looking, and he crawled in. She had no sooner tucked him in and kissed him upon the forehead than he had fallen straight to sleep.

She found Soong and Fray Villadiego standing in the main room.

"He's asleep now," she said, taking a place by the open window.

"Good. We'll let him sleep as long as possible." Soong stroked his moustache as he turned to the priest. "And tell me, Father, what do you plan to do now? The afternoon is free."

"I think," said the Jesuit in his soft voice, "that I will go in search of a chapel in which to give thanks for our safe arrival, and to pray also for the souls of those lost on our journey."

"A good idea," Soong said heartily.

He watched the priest leave, and when no one was about, he turned to Spring Rain and saw the same suspicion in her eyes as his.

"Don't trust him, do you?"

"No, General Soong, I do not."

"Nor I, my child. I trust we should keep our eye on him."

"Just in case," she added solemnly.

"Precisely."

19

Ty-Sun awoke sometime in the early evening. Drowsily he looked about the unfamiliar room, not sure at first where he was. He waited for the bed to move under him, but when it remained perfectly still, he knew he was no longer on the sea but on land, and then he remembered that he was in the English palace.

He yawned, threw back the covers and rose. He crossed over to the windows and pushed aside a curtain. He saw lights on the two junks, but otherwise the river was a ribbon of darkness.

For a few minutes he continued staring out at the pinpricks of light. He was in England now, one of the last reasonable places in which he could look for his empress. Would he find her here? He had a certain feeling about the country, more than he had about any of the others, but whether that was a true feeling or simply residue left from the previous attacks, he didn't know. Since he had come to the palace, he had sensed a certain power that emanated from some unseen source. He had taken a long look at each person he met and wondered which one possessed it. Was it the king? The queen? Or the genial man in green? Or indeed, was it someone he hadn't yet met? He shrugged and spun away from the window.

He paused before a full mirror and studied himself. His body had grown lean in the months since they'd left home, and he marvelled at its new strength. There were hollows in his cheeks where none had existed before. He sighed. Still, he rather thought he preferred being home, listening to *qin* music and being fed sugared almonds. Ah, well, perhaps soon he *would* be home.

Carefully Ty-Sun dressed in one of his newest robes, one of aqua silk with embroidery sewn in gold thread, and in the next room he found Soong and Spring Rain quietly talking.

"You shouldn't have let me sleep so long," he said in an accusing tone.

"You needed the sleep," Spring Rain said, quite unabashed. The dog, Ch'u, was curled into a tight ball, asleep in her lap. At that moment the dog opened his eyes and barked once in greeting, then fell back to sleep.

Ty-Sun noticed that someone had brought in the crystal

containing the pearls. Doubtless it had been Soong, as a reminder not to lose track of time.

"Sleep's good for you," the general said, stretching out his legs as he stroked his moustache. "Besides, we would have come in soon to wake you. We're to dine with Their Majesties in about an hour."

"Excellent, and then we can discuss the details of the ball."

"Lord Elphinstone said he would return in time to escort us," Spring Rain said.

"What do you think of him?" he asked Soong.

"I like him. Seems to have a good head on his shoulders. Doesn't take a lot of this nonsense seriously, which is good."

"Umm, yes."

Someone knocked on the door. A servant sprang forward, opened the door and bowed low as Lord Elphinstone entered.

"Are you ready?" he asked pleasantly, after greeting each one. He had changed clothing and was attired in rose-colored satin.

"Indeed, we are," Ty-Sun answered, and they left for their dinner.

Over the course of the next few days, Lord Elphinstone proved himself an affable guide as he showed Ty-Sun, General Soong, and Spring Rain about the dozens of rooms in the palace. Often Martin joined them, and while the boy remained silent generally, he watched Spring Rain most of the time. In fact the only time the youth spoke was when he was helping the girl with her English.

Hotspur Palace, the Englishman explained, had once been owned by Sir Henry Percy, son of the first earl of Northumberland. His daring and impetuosity in fighting in France earned him the nickname "Hotspur," but before the house was finished, he died in battle. The house remained neglected during the years of the Plantagenets and Tudors, and it was only in the past fifty years that the Crown had acquired it. James I had found it a pleasant change from his other London residences, and thus had begun expanding the building into the present immense structure.

"It's quite impressive," Ty-Sun said as they wandered through a huge hall, some three stories high. Tapestries, all produced in France their guide said, decorated the three walls, while one entire wall was devoted to floor-to-ceiling windows. The spring morning light flooded the room, dazzling them with its brightness, and once they retreated to a room where they could see more clearly, Ty-Sun asked if Lord Elphinstone would be available to show them some of London.

"Of course, Your Majesty," the Englishman said with a bow, "I would be delighted. You have only to let me know when you wish to tour the city, and I will be most happy to escort you."

"Perhaps in a few days," Ty-Sun suggested. "That's long before the ball, and so we have much time to spare and see the sights. I must admit that I didn't see much of Muscovy."

"There wasn't much to see, after all," Soong replied gloomily.

"Ah, yes, so I understand from my fellow countrymen whose adventures have led them to Russland. It is a wild country, and neither the landscape nor the inhabitants are fully tamed."

Ty-Sun chuckled. "I think not. We were given to understand that our departure would be appreciated when I made an unfortunate remark about the . . . size . . . of the women."

"Ah," Elphinstone said, his eyes twinkling, "they weren't petite, then?"

"No, not at all."

They were strolling through a long gallery lined on either side with paintings of royalty for the past several hundred years. Occasionally Soong would stop to stare at one, then move on to another picture.

"You've spoken little of your journey, Your Majesty, and I sense that all has not gone well for you. Is that correct?"

"You are very astute, my lord." The other man gave a slight bow in Ty-Sun's direction. "Yes, much happened that we have kept to ourselves. I do not think my general would mind if I spoke frankly with you. I feel, somehow, that I can trust you."

Ty-Sun clasped his hands behind his back and glanced out a tall window nearby. He could see the palace's formal gardens, which Elphinstone said he would guide them through in the next few days. As to his story . . . should he trust the man and tell him everything? And yet he betrayed nothing by relating their hardships thus far, and he did not think that Elphinstone was an agent for the Enemy. He did not feel it.

"When I arrived," Ty-Sun said, "you heard my reason for coming West, and yet it has not been an easy journey. Not at all, my lord, and by that, I do not mean only that it has been difficult to find the proper woman." He sighed deeply, then launched into a recounting of the tale. He watched the Englishman's face during the story and realized that Elphinstone's expression was not one of disbelief, even when Ty-Sun told about the half-fish creatures and the firebirds. All the better, he thought. When he was finished, he looked at the other man.

"Truly incredible," Elphinstone said after a moment's silence.

"Do you believe me?"

"I have no reason to disbelieve you. I, too, have sensed a growing power . . . an evil that exists in this country, and now, I see, in others as well. You think that if the dragons are killed, then the world will cease to exist?"

"It is a legend in my country, but more than that, too."

"Then we must do all that we can to protect them—and to find you a bride quickly. I will speak to Their Majesties about having the ball a few days earlier. I think that's all they'll agree to."

"I thank you, my lord."

Elphinstone bowed. He glanced around. "Ah, I see Martin is with Spring Rain again. You know, he fancies the girl, and I haven't the heart to explain what a concubine is."

"That is not approved of in England, is it? You were quick to divert the queen's attention from it."

"It is not a Christian belief," Elphinstone said, his voice ironic.

Ty-Sun lifted his eyebrows in surprise. "And you are not a Christian, Lord Elphinstone?"

"Not precisely, Your Majesty."

And with that cryptic remark, the Englishman brought his charges together and guided them through the palace for the remainder of the afternoon.

20

The following day Ty-Sun took Lord Elphinstone and King Charles aboard his ships so that they might inspect them. He introduced the two men to the bear, who did a curious thing, or so Ty-Sun thought.

The bear, already looking far less matted and far more healthy since leaving Russland, lumbered up to Lord Elphinstone, all the while Charles was retreating, and rearing up, placed an immense paw on the man's shoulder. Elphinstone showed no fear, but instead talked to the beast as if it could understand his words. After a moment, the bear seemed to nod its head, and then it went down on all fours again and was led below.

Ty-Sun studied Elphinstone thoughtfully, but made no comment about this incident, beyond saying that the Englishman seemed to have a way with animals.

Elphinstone merely smiled.

Charles asked to see the junks asail, and so Ty-Sun ordered the sailors to cast off. As they sailed up the Thames, away from Hotspur, Ty-Sun stood by a railing and stared about at the city.

London was not very large, at least along the riverfront, and he was surprised. He had expected a monster city, stretching far into the countryside, but as yet it hadn't grown much farther than its original town walls.

Thus, it didn't take long for *The Water Dragon* to move away from central London, and soon King Charles was pointing out Fulham Palace, the summer residence of the London bishops for hundreds of years, and then beyond that on the left bank, the Church of All Saints, with a tower dating from the fifteenth century. Farther down was Barn Elms, a mansion owned by Sir Francis Walsingham of the previous century. The immense and very old elms lining the river lent the estate its name.

There were other great homes and estates, and ancient ruins, as well, to look at, but finally in late morning *The Water Dragon* turned back and returned to London. From what Ty-Sun saw of the countryside beyond the banks of the river he thought it a pleasant land with its rolling hills and great woods.

Once the junk was docked, the men returned to the palace, and there Charles invited Ty-Sun to sit in on his afternoon sessions with his advisors. Ty-Sun said he was honored, and the remainder of his day was spent with the king.

That night nightmares awoke Ty-Sun, and he lay in bed, feeling the sweat pour from his body. He couldn't remember what had frightened him in his dream, and yet he was reluctant to return to sleep. Finally, toward morning, he dropped off.

The next night the dreams returned. Ty-Sun awoke, his heart hammering, and lay in the darkness, which seemed to have changed texture while he slept. It reminded him of the darkness that had almost overwhelmed him at home, and that which he'd encountered on that strange plane. He thought he smelled a faint odor, but he couldn't distinguish the smell. He listened for any alien sound in the room, but heard nothing beyond his own rasping breath and a low growling. He sat up and reached down to the foot of the bed, where Ch'u lay. The dog's fur was bristled along its neck, and he knew the dog's lips were pulled back in a silent snarl.

So, he had not simply imagined . . . it . . . whatever that was. Ch'u had felt it, too. He stroked and patted the dog until the animal finally relaxed. As Ty-Sun looked about the dark bedroom, he wondered what it was that came to him in the night. Whatever it was, he knew why they came.

Finally, the dog curled up alongside his hip, and Ty-Sun lay back again. Although he closed his eyes, he did not go back to sleep.

Nightly the dreams continued, robbing him of his much-needed sleep, and as he moved about in the daytime, he felt as if he were sleepwalking. Sometimes he could hardly keep his eyes open, sometimes he could barely understand what others said, and yet he refused to say anything to Soong or Spring Rain about the terrible dreams. After all, what could they do? This was something he must do on his own.

On the fifth night he awoke, and this time he was not in his bedroom.

He was standing on the plane he had visited before, and he wondered how he had come to be there when he hadn't used the Orb of White Jade. As he stood there, orange lightning arced high above his head, its electrifying fingers spreading out, pulsing downward toward him. He flung himself forward, just as the lightning reached the spot where he had been standing only a moment before. He rolled to the left as the lightning hit again, the ground sizzling from the impact. Then, leaping to his feet, he reached for Dragon's Tongue. Only the sword wasn't at his side.

Never before had he come to the astral plane without his sword. He was weaponless.

And the Enemy knew it.

The lightning forked into three dazzling prongs, then spun quickly until it was a blur of light that throbbed and pulsed, gaining new strength, new deadly intent, with each revolution. Balls of orange lightning shot at him, and he dodged them left and right, ducking and rolling whenever the lightning swerved toward him.

The lightning chased him across the plane, and finally he rolled into a slight recess, and gasped for air. He was growing tired, and before long he'd be unable to do anything. He got to his feet, and stood facing in the direction from which the lightning came. He wasn't completely helpless, at least not yet. He raised his arms and murmured.

He would stop the lightning now. It would be rendered harmless. It couldn't hurt him. After all, this was only a dream, wasn't it? It was only—

Suddenly a shimmering wall of lightning burst around him, then slammed into him, burning each part of him it touched. His skin and hair ignited, and pain seared through his entire being, and he woke, shouting. Lights moved in his bedroom, and he cried out again, only to fall back on the bed when he saw it was Soong and Spring Rain, both with candles. They set them down and crossed quickly to the emperor.

"What's wrong, my lord?" the concubine asked, kneeling by him on the bed. "You were shouting and thrashing. We thought someone had snuck into your room and was attacking you."

"Something was here, after me," he said hoarsely as if his throat hurt.

"Bring him something to drink, Spring Rain," Soong said, and slipped a strong arm around Ty-Sun's shoulders so that he could sit up. In the dim candlelight Soong saw that soot darkened the emperor's face, and that some of his hair had been singed. Soong frowned. What had been going on here?

Spring Rain returned quickly with wine and helped Ty-Sun

bring the goblet to his mouth. His hand shook so much, she had to guide it.

Prudently Soong waited until Ty-Sun had finished the wine, then indicated that Spring Rain should get some more. She had slipped off the bed once more and headed out of the room, when Ty-Sun made a slight gesture with his hand that stopped her.

"No, that's all right. I don't need any more." He pushed himself up, then brushed back his hair from his face. Some of the singed hair came off in his hands, and he glanced at it ruefully.

"What happened?" Soong demanded.

"I had a dream. Or rather at the time, I didn't think it was a dream, but rather reality. I was once more on the astral plane, and all around me was lightning. It was trying to strike me, almost as if it were alive. Finally, it hit me and I began burning, and that's when I awoke." He shuddered.

Thoughtfully Soong stroked his moustache. "There's something bad here in the palace. I've sensed it since we first arrived, but I don't know what it is. Do you, Your Majesty?"

Ty-Sun shook his head.

"What are we to do?" Spring Rain asked. "We cannot leave him alone to sleep now; we cannot trust his dreams any longer."

"That's true. We'll have to take turns—either you or me, Spring Rain, or one of the servants. But we can't trust anyone else." He realized that they were speaking as if Ty-Sun wasn't with them. He glanced at the man, who sat hunched over, his eyes fixed on some distant point. No, they couldn't leave him alone. Not any longer.

"I don't know what's here in the palace—or London—but we'll have to find it first, before it finds us." He left the rest unspoken.

21

There had been great evil afoot last night. He had felt it stirring, as if from some slumber of its own, and his own sleep had been disturbed by odd dreams. Late in the night, he had awakened, shaking slightly from fear and completely drenched in his sweat. He had not been able to sleep for the rest of the night, and so had decided to go out for a brisk walk. Perhaps that would make him feel better.

Now, in the light of early morning Elphinstone strolled through the palace gardens and hoped that the dreams of the previous night would fade from his mind. He had been out nearly an hour when he came to the old tree and stopped by its massive trunk. He ran his hand down the bark, feeling its rough texture. It was the only oak left here, the others having long ago been cut down. Once this area known as London had been filled with the trees, sacred to his religion. Once, long ago.

He sat on the stone bench beneath the tree and leaned his head back against the trunk, feeling the spirit of the tree pulse beneath the bark.

Once, too, there had been many of his religion, with numerous priests, both male and female, and celebrants, and it had been the religion of Britain. Their ceremonies had been rich and frequent, and the wholeness with nature had been complete. But that had been centuries ago, and since the Roman conquest, Druidism had been steadily declining. Too, the trees fell steadily beneath the blade of progress and now, the number of Druids, like those of the trees, was greatly diminished.

As far as he knew, he was the only Druid remaining in this part of England. The others he had known during his long life had fled to the sparsely populated countryside, areas where they hoped they would not be further disturbed.

Perhaps he should have gone, too, and sought a quieter life, and yet he had always liked London, even when it was a raw town, little more than mud-and-wattle huts set in a marshy area. It had an energy unlike any other town in the country, and he had enjoyed seeing it develop with each new reign.

He shifted and sighed. Being by the tree these past few minutes, being outside had helped, and yet the memories of his dreams would not fade. Would they ever, he wondered? He closed his eyes against the images of the orange lightning and of the eyes that seemed to pursue him across some plain. He had never been in that dream-world before, and it disturbed him that he had been taken there against his will.

What evil had been stirred, and how? He had felt only a little disturbance before the arrival of the Emperor Ty-Sun, but since that time he'd sensed a change. Day by day the evil strengthened. He knew it did not feed off of Ty-Sun, nor was Ty-Sun the source of the evil. Rather, the evil was something that pursued the man. He had known this before the emperor had even confided in him.

What was it? Where was it?

There was something different, too, that he had felt recently . . . something that seemed to cause the evil to tremble, if his senses were at all accurate, and they had never betrayed him before.

Something . . . or rather someone . . . at Court, he thought, who disturbed the other side, and he wondered just who that might be. There were hundreds of possibilities, and he would have to narrow it down.

And he would have to watch Ty-Sun, and help him prepare for the evil.

Cromwell watched as the tall foreigner smiled at some small joke the king had just made. This evening the royal couple were giving a dinner in honor of their guests, and Cromwell, as a member of Parliament, had been invited, and now that he was here it was all he could do not to stare at that man. Ty-Sun, he called himself, and Cromwell's lips lifted in a bitter smile.

The man was nothing but trouble, and something had to be done about him.

The first thing Cromwell knew he could do was meet later that evening with his friend, Miles Dunncaster, who had been out of London since the stranger had arrived. They had many things to discuss, among them their common religious beliefs, but tonight they would also be discussing this emperor of the Land of Ten Thousand Willows.

This pagan. With his young concubine and old-man general.

Cromwell glanced down the long table and saw that Lord

Elphinstone, seated not too far from the king, had raised his head and was looking around with a puzzled expression on his face.

Cromwell smiled.

There would be something for *him* as well.

Footsteps echoed behind him, and Ty-Sun paused to listen. He had left the dinner party just minutes ago. It was late in the evening, and many of the lords and ladies had drunk so much that they were no longer being discreet with their conversation. The room was stuffy, and he had had a thundering headache, so he had slipped outside onto the terrace for fresh air.

As he moved away from the palace, he glanced upward. He could see the stars faintly, as if clouds covered the sky. He knew there was a lot of smoke in London—he could smell, even when inside the palace—and combined with the fog from the river, it often obscured the night sky. A pity, he thought, because he enjoyed gazing at the stars. He would have to go outside the city one night to see if he recognized any of the stars.

It was brisk tonight, with no wind, and the air smelled good, much better than what had been inside. Why the English liked stuffy rooms, overheated with candles and far too many bodies, he didn't know. Their food, too, left something to be desired. He thought there was altogether too much emphasis on game meats at their meals, and even that seemed scarcely or unevenly cooked, although usually a rich sauce hid that from the diner.

Still, he had enjoyed sampling the many different foods, many of which were completely new to him, and had found he particularly liked the wines. Perhaps that contributed to his headache, he thought with a suggestion of a smile.

He was heading toward the gardens, which reminded him of how much he missed his own Garden. In a few days the citizens of the Willow Garden would celebrate the Festival of Music, and he wondered how the preparations were going.

He remembered past festivals, and how one year when he had been prince he had gone boating on Willow Lake. A barge, decorated with flowers and vines, carrying his best imperial musicians, had followed, and as he lay back on pillows and gazed up into the starry night, he had listened to the soft strains floating toward him. That had been a good festival.

His mind was turned now to thoughts of home, and he

wondered how Quiet Rabbit was handling the daily affairs that arose. He hoped all was going well. His chamberlain was a good man, always dependable, and so he knew that everything was as it should be. Thank the gods, he had one less worry there.

He should have gone back to his apartments, he thought suddenly, and brought Ch'u out for a walk. The dog hadn't been outside since they'd arrived. Perhaps when he toured London, he would take him along.

Some distance away he saw a tall tree outlined in the moonlit garden against the black backdrop of night, and as he headed toward it, he heard the ghostly footsteps again. Once more he paused, but whoever was following him also paused. He waited, and when the steps did not resume, he continued on his way to the tree. He stopped when he reached it.

An oak of venerable age, he would judge from the tree's girth. He touched the uneven bark, and felt a tingling beneath his fingertips. It was almost as if the tree lived beyond its plant existence; almost as if there were a *spirit* living within it.

Behind him the footsteps quickened, then blurred, and at the last moment Ty-Sun whirled to face whoever had been following him. Something snarled hideously, and then a dog as black as the night but with eyes like dying embers leaped at him.

Just in time he threw up his arm over his face to protect it, then with all his force flung the dog away from him before its teeth clamped down on his arm. At once it leaped back to its feet and attacked him again, and this time Ty-Sun kicked at it with all his strength. He did not wear Dragon's Tongue in the palace, because no one was permitted to wear weapons in the presence of the king, and thus he was unarmed. He had thought earlier about slipping a dagger into a pocket, but had forgotten in his haste to get to the dining hall.

Now, he faced the dog without any steel weapon. The animal stood only a few feet away and growled low in its throat. So far he had managed not to be bitten, although he thought the dog's teeth had scraped along his wrist when he was protecting his face. The dog, which he saw now came almost to his waist, watched him, waiting, and in that moment as Ty-Sun raised his hand, the dog launched itself at him.

Blue lightning burst in front of the dog, and it shrieked, then pulled back before it was burned. The lightning died down, and Ty-Sun retreated a few steps and watched his adversary.

This was no ordinary dog; this was something more . . . something sent by the Enemy.

Deep in its throat, threatening, the dog growled again, and advanced, its legs curiously stiff. White drool dripped from its mouth, and when it opened its jaws, Ty-Sun could see the double row of white and extremely sharp teeth.

This time, he thought, the dog wouldn't be playing with him. This time the creature would go for his throat. He backed up slowly, hoping to gain some more time. The animal's eyes never moved from him. He had to do something before it leaped.

Too late! The dog sprang forward, its mouth wide open, the glistening fangs ready, but Ty-Sun moved his hands, and clouds just the size of the dog formed over the creature, and rain poured down on it. The rain slammed into the dog, flattening it against the ground with its watery assault. The rain pounded against the unnatural dog, and it howled in pain.

Momentarily Ty-Sun felt anguish that the animal was hurt. He had never harmed an animal before, but then he remembered this was not a real dog, not like his little Ch'u. The dog bayed again, the deep sound sending icy prickles across the back of Ty-Sun's neck. He leaned forward and murmured a few words, and the rainfall quickened.

The rain seemed to be keeping the dog from moving toward him, and Ty-Sun decided he had seen enough of the gardens by moonlight. With as much dignity as he could muster, he picked up his robes and rushed back toward the palace. When he was within sight of the door, he turned back to the garden and removed the rain spell. He wondered if the dog was alive, or if it had been knocked unconscious. He listened, but heard nothing. With a shiver, he turned toward the door.

"Your Majesty."

Startled, Ty-Sun leaped backward, then recognized the voice of Fray Villadiego. He had been taken completely unaware when the man had stepped out of the shadows toward him.

"Your Majesty, are you all right?"

"Yes, yes, Fray." Ty-Sun took a deep breath. "You just startled me."

The priest bowed, as if in apology. "I am very sorry, Your

Majesty. I noticed that you were gone, and came out to see if you were all right."

"I'm fine, really. It was too warm inside, and I thought I would go for a brief walk."

"I trust you are feeling much better now?"

"Much."

Fray Villadiego waited until Ty-Sun went in, then he followed discreetly behind. On the stone terrrace, where the priest had been standing, a small puddle of water glistened.

22

When he returned to the dining hall, Ty-Sun slipped back unnoticed, or so he thought, into his place. When he was able to, though, Soong got up and came over to him, and strongly expressed his blunt disapproval of Ty-Sun for having slipped away for a few minutes, and reminded him that he might well be in danger at the palace. Ty-Sun simply shrugged and tried to ignore the slight throbbing in his left arm.

Later, back in his apartments and alone, he pulled his sleeve up away from his wrist and gazed down at the long raw marks in his skin. He heard the hiss of drawn-in breath and looked up to see Spring Rain staring down at the scratches. Hastily he pushed his sleeve down.

"How did you get those, my lord?"

"I think I must have scratched myself while I was out walking earlier. A thorn bush, perhaps."

Her eyes were wide, her expression steady, and he knew she didn't believe him.

"You should have that washed out, my lord. Scratches can be serious." Somewhat abashed, he nodded. "Wait one moment, and I will clean the wound so that it will not become infected."

Wound, he thought, not cut. He waited until she returned with a basin of warm water, and soft strips of cloth. She dabbed gently at the scratches, washing away the bits of blood, and then patted the area dry. She then daubed a salve onto the area, which was now swelling slightly. Ty-Sun flinched; the salve stung.

"It serves you right, my lord," Spring Rain said severely. "You leave without telling us where you are going, and then you are injured in some encounter in the garden."

His eyes closed, he did not correct her. Why bother, when he knew she was right?

She tapped him on the chest with a small finger, and as he opened his eyes, she leaned close to him.

"You could have been hurt far worse . . . or even killed tonight, and we wouldn't have been able to help you at all. You mustn't wander around by yourself any longer, my lord. Too much depends on your well-being. Please, promise me that you will not."

"You're right," he said, "and I won't."

"Promise?"

"Yes."

She began bandaging his wrist, and he marvelled at the deftness of her hands. She could have been a healer, he thought, because in that field her peasant origins would not have mattered. She was wonderfully provided with common sense, too, and was always eager to learn. He decided that when they returned home, he would suggest that she study to be a healer. He would release her as his concubine, albeit somewhat reluctantly, and she could study about ointments and herblore. There were many women physicians in the Garden, many famous ones in history. Had not his own ancestor, the Warlord Empress, been a woman physician? Spring Rain would make an excellent one, with her strong capable hands and her sympathetic ways. Yes, he rather liked that idea, and he thought she might, too, although he knew he would miss her. But perhaps she could become his court physician.

He reached out with his good hand and cupped the girl's chin in his fingers. Then he bent down and kissed her warm lips.

"Ah, but, my lord," she said with a delightfully mischievous smile, "you are terribly wounded tonight and must rest."

"Not *that* wounded," he said, and falling back onto the bed, pulled her down to him.

Each night his royal hosts provided hours of entertainment, which Ty-Sun found much more interesting than that buffoonery he'd seen in Muscovy. Here he saw masques and plays such as the *Faerie Queene*, and witnessed equally remarkable singers. Henrietta Maria confided that until only a few years ago actresses had no part in plays; all roles being played by men or boys. But then a French actress appeared at Blackfriars, and just recently the queen had brought some actresses from France and was herself rehearsing a part in a masque.

Too, Ty-Sun listened to the delightfully lilting music played on hautboys, virginals, lutes, harps and recorders, as well as numerous other instruments, many of them previously unknown to him. He then instructed Spring Rain and the few musicians left in his entourage to play some of the more traditional music from their country, and when they were finished, they were roundly applauded by the English.

Inadvertently, Ty-Sun also introduced tea to the court. One afternoon Elphinstone had entered the emperor's apartments to find Soong, Ty-Sun and Spring Rain drinking a pale liquid that was not alcohol. With a smile, Ty-Sun had offered some to the English lord, who promptly declared it an excellent beverage. Shortly after that, Charles asked Ty-Sun if he might sample some of the new "chai," or tea. Of course, Ty-Sun graciously agreed, and educated the king and queen in its preparation. The new drink became an instant success, and Ty-Sun noted to Soong that this might well be the start of a prosperous trade between England and the Garden.

Despite the various court amusements, which often lasted into the early morning hours, Ty-Sun found he had time to do other things. And one of those things which he enjoyed most was to stroll through the gardens now that the weather was turning warmer.

Since that nighttime encounter with the black dog, he had not returned to the gardens, but, finally, one day, he told himself he was being foolish in denying himself an enjoyment. Thus, he dressed in a magnificent robe of crimson silk and proceeded to go outside. Ch'u, who had grown even fatter with the English food, ran on his short legs by his master's side. He had persuaded Soong not to accompany him, saying he did not think anything would happen to him in the daytime. It was only at night, or so it seemed thus far, that the Enemy moved against him. Reluctantly Soong had agreed.

How the English love their gardens, Ty-Sun thought, as he stared at the carefully pruned trees and shrubs. Or at least, their monarchs did. He did not think formal gardens would be found at many houses in London.

White gravel filled the paths between the extensive flowerbeds, and it crunched slightly underfoot as he walked. He had to stop from time to time to let Ch'u catch up or rest a little. The tiny dog ran with his tongue hanging out, and Ty-Sun smiled at the sight.

Spring flowers—narcissus, crocus, snowbells, jonquils and daffodils—were up, nodding their bright petals in the slight wind. Here and there, he saw tiny buds forming on the branches of bushes and trees, buds that would soon burst into bloom. He recognized azalea and the scrawny, leafless bushes of roses.

So many flowers yet to bloom, he thought, and decided that

not only would he export tea, he would send along some of his most select flowers. It would be interesting to see what plants thrived here.

He missed the Garden, missed the riot of colors and the blend of fragrances that would surround the palace now, and he hoped that he would soon find his empress and return home. Each day he rose and looked at the growing pile of pearls in the bottom of the crystal. Only a few days ago Lord Elphinstone had reported that he'd had no success in persuading the English royal couple to schedule the ball a little earlier than planned. They said simply that it couldn't be done, and that, Elphinstone said wryly, had been that.

Time was running out. Soong reminded him of *that* constantly, and yet what was he to do?

And then today, for some reason, he was extremely tired—perhaps it was because he had been up until well after four in the morning discussing poetry with Lord Elphinstone and several friends of his, and now the warmth of the spring sunshine wasn't making it any easier for him. He yawned, blinked sleepily. If he wasn't careful he would end up taking a nap on a garden bench. Perhaps he should go back to the palace; decidedly a nap was long overdue.

Ty-Sun paused. Had he heard singing?

Intrigued, he scanned the large expanse of palace garden, past the trimmed hedges, many of which reached far above his head, yet could see no one else nearby, beyond one or two gardeners. And certainly they were not the source of that beguiling song.

Had he heard it, though? Perhaps it was only some trick of the wind.

No, there it was again!

He glanced down at Ch'u, whose head was cocked at the distant sound. No, he hadn't imagined it after all. As he listened to the snatches of lilting music wafted to him by the wind, Ty-Sun relaxed. With each passing moment, his exhaustion and worries melted away, almost as if by magic. He felt invigorated, fresh, as though he had slept a week and had awakened a newly born man. He was ready to meet anything the Enemy sent his way!

Ty-Sun hurried back the way he had progressed through the garden. He must find the singer, a woman or young boy, he judged, from the high sound. As he walked quickly, almost running, down the paths of white gravel, the stones flung up behind him. Ch'u, long tongue lolling, raced at his heels. He thought the music came from his right now, and so he searched through the maze that stood there, then rushed past the line of hedges in the topiary. But he couldn't find the singer.

It was, he thought, almost as if the singer were deliberately eluding him, and yet that wasn't possible. Or was it?

Every so often, when he paused, he would hear a few notes drifting to him, and once more he would renew his search.

But as an hour passed, and he was not successful in locating the source, Ty-Sun stopped to rest. An exhausted Ch'u collapsed at his feet.

The singing had stopped. There would be no more today, he knew.

But, he thought with a smile, there was always tomorrow.

When Ty-Sun returned to his apartments some time later, he related the extraordinary incident of the unseen singer in the garden to Soong and asked him what he thought of it.

The general stroked his moustache and gazed thoughtfully into the distance. "'You received no bad . . . impression . . . of it, Your Majesty?"

Ty-Sun shook his head. "No, none at all. It was as if my very spirit had been renewed while I was listening. Ch'u was even wagging his tail." He paused, then frowned. "You don't think it's some trick of the Enemy's, do you, Soong?"

"No. This isn't like the song of those fish-creatures we encountered in the Great Ice, but rather something healing. That's a good sign, and very unusual, too. I think we should find the singer as soon as possible."

"You think that—"

Soong held up a hand to quell the other's eagerness. "Your Majesty, I think nothing beyond that we should find this singer."

Ty-Sun nodded. Soong was right. He shouldn't try to make too much of something he knew nothing of. They would wait, would find the singer, and then— He didn't know what would happen then.

He knew that he should lie down for a nap, even though he felt refreshed, and so he excused himself. While he slept, his dreams were marked by the song he had heard such a short time before. Its notes rippled through his mind, caressing him, beckoning him.

When Ty-Sun awoke a short time later, he was surprised to find himself alone. He could have sworn that someone had been sitting by his bed looking at him just a moment before.

But, doubtless, that had been Spring Rain, he told himself as he rose, and found himself oddly disappointed by the thought. He didn't want it to be her; he wanted it to be . . . who he wanted there he didn't know.

23

The next day when Ty-Sun was free of any social commitments he excused himself and went directly to the garden and wandered slowly through the paths, hoping he would hear the singer again. But he did not. The day after followed the same pattern, as did the day after that, and the next day.

Each afternoon he waited patiently for the singer to begin, but he did not hear her—he had decided it wasn't a young boy he'd heard—again.

One day Ty-Sun asked Lord Elphinstone if he knew of any woman at Court who possessed a most remarkable voice, and although the Englishman had looked at him a little curiously, he'd replied that he knew no woman with the quality of voice Ty-Sun described. Ty-Sun said he would appreciate it greatly if Elphinstone heard the singer that he would send for him at once.

Elphinstone agreed.

"She's gone," Ty-Sun remarked mournfully one evening to Soong. He had been out in the gardens all afternoon, and was looking far healthier than he had for some time. He had color to his cheeks, and while his hair was a little wind-blown, Soong didn't think it would harm him. "Gone, before I even knew her."

"Perhaps she has little reason to sing now."

"Perhaps." Ty-Sun did not sound wholly convinced by the other's argument.

Soong tried hard not to smile at his emperor's mournful tone, but was not altogether successful. He covered it by coughing.

"I would suggest, Your Majesty, that you wait a few more days before you begin to despair, and if you still do not hear her, I will begin making discreet inquiries. Perhaps you have heard a servant girl singing while she worked. If that is so, I do not think Lord Elphinstone would have any knowledge of her or of her ability. In the meantime, you must rest."

"Yes, yes, I've no doubt you're right." Ty-Sun's tone was absent, as if his thoughts already lay elsewhere, and indeed they were once more joined with the lilting notes of the enchanting song.

Would he, he wondered, ever hear the singer again? And if he didn't, how could he ever tolerate living without the song?

From the window in her room overlooking the gardens Spring Rain sat and watched as Ty-Sun strode down the white paths between the flowerbeds. For the last week he had been intent—even insistent—upon going alone to the gardens each afternoon at a certain hour, and once when she had asked if she could go with him, he had fairly shouted at her that he wanted to be alone. Each day she watched as he poked under trees and around bushes, looked into various outbuildings, investigated every turn, every inch of the garden, almost as if he were looking for something . . . for someone.

This pattern repeated itself without fail every day, and once it was completed, he would start it again, until hours later, he would seem to give up.

A terrible sadness filled Spring Rain, because she knew what Ty-Sun was searching for, and she knew that, as much as she loved him, she would never be able to give it to him, though she desired to.

Soon . . . all too soon . . . her lord would find his bride, his empress, and her life would change. While she might continue as the respected concubine, she would only be that . . . a concubine. A well-loved companion of former days.

Yet, because she loved him, she would do all she could to help her lord and his prospective bride. She would do nothing to harm them, only to aid them.

Tears filling her eyes, she turned away from the window.

"Yes, Mr. Cromwell?" King Charles asked wearily. "What is it you wish?" He left the words "this time" unspoken. Cromwell had requested to see Charles privately, and so the king had permitted him to come to his writing closet, where only a handful of his closest advisors would be present.

"Your Majesty, I have come to discuss with you a matter of great import." The Puritan's homely face wore its usual grave expression.

All the matters about which Cromwell came to see the king were important. Or so Cromwell claimed, Charles thought with a suppressed grin. He glanced at one of his advisors, who raised an eyebrow.

"Yes?" Charles really didn't want to hear what Cromwell had to say. He had heard this sort of thing many times over, and he was thoroughly disgusted with the man his wife called an ugly little gnome.

"It is about that evil man."

"Which one is that, pray tell?" Charles sighed to himself. Cromwell could well be talking about any member of the Court, all of whom the Puritan had denounced at one time or the other as utterly frivolous and completely devoid of moral sense. Which many were, the king would concede, although not all. Certainly Lord Elphinstone had a good head on his shoulders.

"The foreigner."

Which one was this? The Court was filled with foreigners, with explorers and ambassadors and poets and such from European courts. Then he realized who Cromwell meant. "The emperor?"

"So he styles himself."

"I think we must take his word for that. What is it about him that . . . offends . . . you?" No doubt Cromwell was offended because the emperor was taller, thinner and much more handsome than he. Cromwell seemed to hate anything that was pleasant; Charles had even heard mutterings of late from the Puritans that the theaters should be closed. What prigs these men were!

Cromwell leaned close. "His very presence here offends me, Your Majesty. That man brings evil and immorality to this country. Have you not seen that woman he calls his concubine? A slattern, as anyone can well see. He claims that he is looking for a bride in our country. How do we know he isn't seeking a woman simply to enslave her with his passions? Why should we sentence some moral Englishwoman to a hell of licentiousness and blasphemy with that . . . man?"

"Cromwell," the king warned, but he knew it would do little good. He had warned the man about his excesses before, but still it did not deter him. Nothing cooled his fanaticism. Was this the sort of ignorance Charles's sister Elizabeth faced in her Bohemian kingdom which was now being torn apart by religious differences?

"You must tell him to depart—nay, you must force him to leave our country at once. The longer he stays, the worse he grows. Already he is preaching the ways of his debased religion with its numerous false gods and profanity. He does not know the way of the True Religion, and for that he is damned, as are all those who listen to him. He knows nothing of decency, of devotion, of all that is good and just." Cromwell's voice dropped to a whisper. "Too, there are rumors, Your Majesty, that the man is in league with Satan. He is said to practice magic, to cast spells. Do you not see how he has enchanted that savage bear?"

"Magic?" Charles's voice held a tone of incredulity. "False gods?"

"Yes, Your Majesty, it is so. He and his bewitched people worship many pagan gods. They know nothing of the True Way, and have even rejected the word of a Christian missionary come to aid in their salvation. He is a harbinger of superstition, of quackery. And while he is here, while we yet tolerate him in our presence, *we* are tainted."

"Good God, tainted? Tainted? You call us that, sir?" Charles's voice was rising dangerously high, and his stammer deepened. "By what right, Mr. Cromwell, do you denounce him?"

"As moral arbitrator of this Court, Your Majesty. The man is an abomination. You must rid yourself of him, before he infects you."

"Get out, Cromwell." The king's face was flushed, and his eyes glittered angrily.

Stunned by the other man's outburst, Cromwell stopped and stared at him. Charles had never reacted this way before.

"Get out at once. I do not wish to see you again today, perhaps even this week." He nodded to his advisors, who stepped forward to assist the Puritan if he should prove reluctant to leave.

But Cromwell knew he had no choice. He took a step back, bowed slightly, then left the king's chamber. He did not look back. The king hated and feared him, but could do nothing because of Cromwell's popularity, and because Cromwell's cause was righteous.

While the king might do nothing about the yellow-skinned foreigner, Cromwell knew others who would. He smiled.

Charles said nothing to his guests of Cromwell's dislike, deeming it of little consequence. He enjoyed the company of the emperor, as did Henrietta Maria, and that was more important than the overblown opinion of some strait-laced Puritan.

And that was where one of his greatest mistakes lay.

* * *

"Something must be done about this intolerable situation," Oliver Cromwell said that evening as he glanced about at his small, close-knit circle of friends.

The men were meeting in defiance of the king's express wishes. On numerous occasions during his reign Charles had made it abundantly clear that he would not tolerate the Puritans gathering publicly or privately. So far, he had not done anything to stop them, but Cromwell and the others knew that would come all too soon.

The yellow light from the fire washed against the plainness of the room, casting the corners in shadows, and it was in one such corner, far darker than the others, that another watched, saying nothing at all. He was ignored by Cromwell's friends, or perhaps they did not see him concealed by the shadows.

"I agree," Miles Dunncaster said without hesitation. "That damned foreigner has swept into Court and in a matter of only a few days has positively beguiled the king. 'Tisn't natural, I tell you." His was a plain face that rarely smiled, and he had short-cropped brown hair and light eyes that could have been green or grey; it was hard to tell sometimes. In his youth he had been slim, but now tended toward stockiness. He owned land to the east of London, and while not rich, lived in fairly comfortable circumstances.

Dunncaster, a fairly influential Puritan, like Cromwell in Parliament, before the king had dismissed Parliament, had brought his three sons with him this evening to participate in the meeting. The two elder ones, Nicholas and Job, were in their early twenties and had the sharp unsmiling features of their father, although youth softened theirs. Both stood well over six feet in their stockinged feet, and were vocal advocates of Puritanism.

The third son, Edmund, was far younger than his brothers, being only eighteen, and his face was less harsh than those of his family. His eyes were a light brown, as was his thick hair, and his mouth had a tendency to curve into a smile, a most inappropriate expression, his father had often reminded him at the wrong end of a birch rod. He was not as tall as his brothers, either, falling some inches short of being six feet, and his views on religion were far more generous than those of his father or brothers.

"Bewitched is more like it," grunted a third man, one John Hartwood. Of the men gathered there he was less inclined to speak out, but obviously tonight he was motivated to do so.

He wore plain, unadorned dark clothes, as did his friends. He was slender, almost to the point of being bony, the youngest of those gathered, although his dark hair was already streaked with grey. Reddish freckles dotted the back of his thin hands, and deep lines were etched between his eyebrows.

"I agree, Mr. Hartwood," Nicholas Dunncaster said. "There's more than meets the eye here."

Elias Summerville nodded his head emphatically, his pink jowls trembling. He was a fairly corpulent man, given to enjoying the good life, despite his current choice of religions. He had come to this religion late in life, having always been a somewhat backsliding Anglican. No one knew how deep his conversion had truly been, although some of the more devout Puritans sometimes questioned his faith.

"Yes, that's so. I think I see the Devil's hand in this matter. What else would explain the king's sudden infatuation with this so-called emperor?"

" 'Tis the hand of the Popish that I see here," Miles Dunncater said. Both Nicholas and Job nodded their agreement. He stood up, locked his hands behind his back and began pacing up and down the room. Several times he passed the corner where the watcher sat, but never once did he glance that way, nor did the watcher even stir as Dunncaster went by.

Summerville slapped his hand down upon the table. "Aye, so it is. I have seen the yellow devils myself in that Godforsaken boat of theirs. And the woman witch, too."

"Aye," said Hartwood, "and I have seen a Catholic priest going aboard the ship as well."

A surprised murmuring rose among the men at this revelation. Only Edmund, sitting at one end of the table, did not join in the discussion, and Miles wondered, not for the first time that night, if he had made a mistake in bringing his youngest son with him. Still, the boy had to learn sometime, and it was good to get him away from his sister and among his father's friends. The boy had too much time to sit and think by himself.

Unity Stoke and Elias Welborne nodded significantly at each other. They could have been twins by their thin plain looks, and some regarded them as simple-minded. Yet they were good men for the most part, although they tended to let others, like Dunncaster and Cromwell, do their thinking for them.

The conversation continued in a heated manner for some time, as the Puritans argued about the very poor influence the foreign emperor might have upon the king, and then finally, Dunncaster surveyed his friends.

"Well, what are we going to do about it? We see there is an evil influence at Court, and the longer we wait, the worse it becomes."

"We should tell the king what we know of the sorcerer," Stoke suggested, while Welborne nodded vigorously. "Perhaps then he would have a change of heart."

"I have already discussed the matter with the king," Cromwell said, "and he would not listen to reason. Indeed, he asked me to leave."

"Whatever we could say wouldn't do any good," Job said, looking around at his elders. "None at all, I fear. The king is well past reasoning; he refuses to listen to anything we've said in the past."

"That's true," Cromwell said as he glanced at the one corner where the watcher sat. "The king believes only what he wishes to—and no amount of persuasion will convince him otherwise."

"Then what?"

"Then, Miles, I suggest that we take a more active part in ridding our king and his Court of this foreign menace."

"You mean—" Dunncaster began.

"Precisely," Cromwell cut him off. "We must kill this so-called emperor and his friends, destroy them before anything happens to us."

24

It had been well over a week since Ty-Sun had heard the beautiful singing, and he was beginning to despair that he would ever hear that voice again. He continued with his various activities, but his thoughts centered almost exclusively on the unseen singer. He must see her.

Each afternoon he returned faithfully to the garden and waited, and finally his persistence was rewarded. Once more he heard the singing.

This time, though, he *would* see the singer, and without wasting a further moment, he rushed toward the sound. Ch'u, who had been trotting at his master's side, suddenly dashed off to the right, cutting across a wide expanse of grass. The dog must know where the woman is, he thought, and he started off across the lawn as well.

The dog disappeared around a tall hedge, and as Ty-Sun got closer, he heard the song more clearly. She was there. Holding his breath slightly, he rounded the corner, and there on a marble bench was a young girl. Ch'u, his head cocked, sat at her feet, while a large tawny hound and a smaller black dog lay stretched out by the bench. A trio of rabbits faced her, while just beyond them a squirrel chittered to no one in particular. Birds of all sizes and colors perched on the branches of nearby twigs. Beside the girl on the bench, methodically washing one white paw, sat a black and white cat. It looked up as Ty-Sun came around the corner of the hedge, and he saw that its eyes were as gold as the sun.

As soon as she saw him, the girl stopped singing and stared at him in amazement. He smiled, thinking how outlandish he must look to her.

"Please, mistress, continue singing. I'm sorry if I frightened you."

"You simply startled me," she said. "You did not frighten me, sir."

"I heard you singing and wanted to see you . . . that is, I heard you another time, and when I thought I might be able to find the source of the beautiful song, I rushed toward the sound. Or rather," he admitted ruefully, "I rushed after my dog, who found you first. That is my dog," he said pointing to Ch'u. The girl's cheeks were flushed a delicate pink, a shade most becoming to her. "I'm sorry, mistress—my manners have suddenly failed me." He bowed low, his eyes on her. "My name is Ty-Sun, and I am emperor of the Land of Ten Thousand Willows."

"I have heard of you, sir," she admitted shyly. She ducked her head, her long hair sliding forward across one cheek. Her speaking voice, unlike her high fluting singing voice, was deeper than he had expected, almost throaty, and the sensual sound of it sent a ripple of excitement through him.

"What is your name?" he asked softly, entranced by the sight of her.

"I am Blessing Dunncaster."

She smiled, and as he returned the smile he gazed at her. She was slender, and her hair, done in hip-length braids, was the most incredible shade of titian. High cheekbones set in an oval face, with a long thin nose, and a slightly pointed chin. Her arched eyebrows were more brown than titian, and she had a small mouth with pink lips, and deep blue eyes that regarded him seriously and shyly, yet without fright.

She wore a grey wool gown of a rather severe cut, with a wide white collar and an apron across the front of her dress. Her unadorned shoes were black leather, and she wore no ornamentation, unlike the other women he'd seen at the English Court. He wondered why she wore such an ugly dress; he would outfit her in an array of golds and apricot, shades that would make her blue eyes stand out even more, and which would glorify her unusual hair. Never grey, though.

Ty-Sun thought Blessing Dunncaster was the most beautiful woman he had ever seen, and oddly enough, he found himself tongue-tied. Not knowing what else to do, he continued gazing at her.

"Please, sit down, sir. Or should I call you 'Your Majesty?' "

"It doesn't matter," he said as he sat on the other side of the cat, who was now licking its other front paw. He turned to look at her, then realized she must think his gaze was rude. He turned away.

"Please, don't."

"What?"

"You don't have to stop looking at me. I . . . like it."

She blushed again, this time more violently, and Ty-Sun found his own cheeks feeling slightly warm. He hadn't felt this way since he'd been a small boy. Whatever was the matter with him? He had to say something. He couldn't just sit here, staring at her.

"Do you come frequently to the gardens?" he finally asked. "I heard you almost two weeks ago, but after that time, I didn't, even though I came every afternoon to listen to your singing."

"You are very kind, Your Majesty."

"I've changed my mind," he said. "Please, just call me Ty-Sun."

"Ty-Sun." She said it aloud and savored the alienness of it. "What does it mean?"

"It means 'the Protector.' "

"I like it. It's a very strong name. Ty-Sun. As to your question . . . I come here occasionally, whenever my father permits me. He is a very strict man and says that the Court is a wicked place, particularly for girls my age."

He looked at the plainness of her hairstyle, of her clothing, and remembered those people whom Lord Elphinstone had pointed out in their travels about London. "Is your father a Puritan?"

"Yes."

"Ah." There was nothing more he could say, for in the short time he had been in England, he did not think he had found a more bigoted group than the Puritans, and he did not wish to hurt the girl.

"It's my father's religion," she said softly, almost as if she had known what he was thinking. "He doesn't like it when I sing, and so I come to the gardens to be alone and to sing."

"Then I should leave you so that you might continue." He started to rise.

"No, please, I can sing while you're here."

"Very well."

She smiled once more and began singing, while Ty-Sun listened, rapt, to the beautiful songs. Many were in an odd language that seemed very old, and without knowing the words, he knew what the songs were about. Love, great battles and greater warriors, gods and goddesses from olden times, a race of people who had forgotten their old ways, turning to a new god.

The sun inched across the sky, sinking toward the west as the shadows around them lengthened and turned a deep purple. Finally, when she was finished, she fell silent. The cat had curled up on her lap, and slowly she stroked it. Ch'u lay sleeping at Ty-Sun's feet, while Ty-Sun stared off into the distance, still lost within the spells of her songs. The last of the daylight glimmered for an instant, then faded quickly.

At last, though, she glanced up, and seeing how late it had grown, she stood up.

"I'm sorry, Your—I mean, Ty-Sun, I must be going. I'm already overdue, long overdue, and my father will be furious."

"May I see you again?" he asked as she picked up the cat and began walking quickly down a path toward the palace.

"Yes, I'll be here tomorrow afternoon at the same time."

"So shall I," Ty-Sun said softly, as he watched her on the path to the palace. When she had gone inside, he returned to the bench. Around him the evening deepened, and still he sat there, deep in thought.

Each afternoon Ty-Sun met with Blessing. No matter how early he arrived, he always found her waiting. And each time he saw her he felt something within him leap like a wild deer. Sometimes she sang for him, again in that oddly stirring language; other times they simply sat and talked.

He asked her about her family, and she replied that she had three brothers and a father, her mother having died when she was just a child. Something in the memory still pained her, so Ty-Sun did not pursue that subject.

"And what of your family? What relatives does an emperor have?" she asked laughingly.

"Alas, I think this one has far too many. I have many aunts and uncles, and cousins, and all of them mean well, but do not seem to like anything that I like. I know that one or two of them hope that I will die without issue so that the throne will pass to them."

Her cheeks turned slighly red. "You do not have children, then."

He smiled. "No, nor a wife."

"Oh."

"And you? Are you engaged?"

She shook her head. "No, my father refuses to allow me to see any suitors at all. He doesn't want it to be pass—I mean, he's very strict." Quickly she looked away in confusion.

Ty-Sun lifted an eyebrow. Her father didn't want something

to be passed along? To her children? That had to be what she meant. He was intrigued, yet knew it wouldn't be polite to pry. Yet . . .

His tone was gentle. "What doesn't your father wish passed along to your children, Blessing? The color of your hair?"

"Don't be absurd!"

"Your blue eyes then?"

She laughed and shook her head. "I can't tell you . . . not today . . . perhaps never."

"Very well, I shall now bore you with the details of my journeys from my land." He spoke of the many sights he had witnessed thus far, then began talking about the Willow Garden. "Spring in the Garden is a beautiful time, and tomorrow would be the Festival of Yellow Birds. Every year a pair of birds with magnificent plumage like the rays of the sun return to the Garden on the same day, and their arrival is celebrated with singing and dancing and much dining."

"It sounds so beautiful. You must miss your home very much."

"I do."

She glanced sidelong at him. "And you still have the bear?"

"Oh, yes. He lives on board *The Water Dragon* and eats a great amount of fish. I think some of the sailors spend all their time finding food for him."

"Will you keep him?"

"If he'll stay with me."

She turned around now to face him. "That's a very strange thing to say, Ty-Sun."

He glanced at the ring of animals that had gathered, as usual, around her. "I would think not. Look at the animals that come to you. They recognize a sympathetic spirit."

"Then you believe that animals are much like people? That they have their likes and dislikes, that they think as we do?"

"Yes."

Her face brightened. "And animals like you, too, Ty-Sun?"

He smiled down at the cat, which had curled up between them. "I think so. I have many pets at home and always seem to be acquiring more. Is there something you wish to tell me, Blessing?"

"Something? What do you mean?" She tried to maintain an innocent look, but failed.

"You have a special way with animals, don't you?" he asked.

"No!" She leaped to her feet, upsetting the cat, who meowed mournfully. "No, I don't!"

Ty-Sun took her hands in his; they were icy, and he tried to warm them with his own.

"It's all right. Please, Blessing, sit down. Here. I didn't mean to upset you."

She sat again and did not try to pull her hands away from his.

"You see, in my country, that's a wonderful ability—to talk to animals, to know their minds." She looked at him. "There are other traits that we don't fear, as other people do."

"I see that now."

"Is there anything that you wish to tell me, Blessing?"

She looked down at the cat, then up at her companion. "Yes, but . . ."

"I won't tell anyone. On my honor."

"Very well." She cleared her throat, then slowly withdrew her hands. "You see, I'm a witch."

25

"A witch." He stared, delighted, at her.

"Yes. But, I've said too much. I must go." She started to get up.

"No, don't, please." He took hold of her arm. She glanced down at it, and he slowly released her. "Please stay, Blessing."

Her eyes wouldn't meet his. "I should not have said anything to you."

"I think it was good that you did. I am a sorcerer," he said with a smile.

"A sorcerer!" She stared in disbelief at him. "No, you couldn't be. I'm the only one with this terrible affliction."

He laughed. "It's not an affliction. It's a wonderful ability."

The color had drained from her. "No, you don't understand, Ty-Sun. It's a terrible thing . . . just like being able to talk with animals. A terrible thing . . . and they could hang me . . . and you . . . if they learned of this."

"They?"

"The authorities."

"You mean, the Puritans." She said nothing, but he knew he was right. "Your father knows, doesn't he?" Her head barely moved. "And so he doesn't want you to marry so that this 'stigma' won't be passed along to your children. And he discourages you from singing because he believes it's part of your being a witch."

"Yes."

He reached out and stroked her cheek. It was so cool to his touch, as if she had turned to marble before his very eyes.

"You mustn't be afraid, Blessing."

"But I am . . . for myself and for you."

"There is someone at Court like us, you know." She looked at him then, disbelief in her eyes. "Yes, there is. A man named Lord Elphinstone. Ah, I see from your expression that you know of him. I sense a power there, and I urge you to trust him if you ever need to talk with someone."

"I don't think we should talk about this any longer," she said.

"Very well. What do you wish to discuss?"

"I don't know. Your land, perhaps. When you spoke of it a little while ago, you sounded so wistful. Will you go back soon?"

"I would like to, but I think not." He thought of the pearls, and how each day added another one to the pile. "I've been away for many months now, and I'm afraid it will still take some time."

"What will take time?"

Even as he opened his mouth to speak, he remembered why he was here. He had forgotten about that while he spent his afternoons with Blessing. He had forgotten about how he was to find a bride; he had not forgotten about love, though, because he thought—no, he knew—he had fallen in love with her. He thought she liked him, but beyond that, he didn't know.

He felt a kinship with her that he had not felt with any other human being in his lifetime. He loved her, but what was he to do? He knew he shouldn't pursue this relationship, which had begun so innocently. If he did, he knew his feelings for her would deepen; yet he could not marry her. Not when he was destined for another bride. There were alternatives, one part of him countered. And those were? She could become one of his concubines, the chief one, at that. She would not agree to that, nor could he usurp Spring Rain from her position of honor. No, there were no alternatives.

What was he to do?

"Is anything wrong, Ty-Sun?" she asked anxiously. Her hand briefly touched the back of his, before she remembered herself and withdrew to sit primly, her hands clasped in her lap.

"No. Yes, I mean. I haven't ever told you the reason I left my beloved country." He sighed. This would not be easy. "I am searching for a bride."

Her lips trembled slightly. "A bride. I see." Her eyes glanced away.

He wished he could take Blessing into his arms, but he could not, because it wouldn't be proper for him, or for her, a gentlewoman. Yet he longed to embrace and kiss her. He closed his eyes.

"But, my search is more complicated than you would guess. The Willow Garden is in peril from some unknown enemy—an enemy who has recently begun making attacks upon it. Upon my birth a prophecy was made that if I did not marry within three years after the death of my father, the dragons who reside in my land would die, and thus my land and the entire earth would be destroyed. And so, before my time runs out, I must find my bride."

"You haven't found her, then."

"She must pass a test, first. We've brought a herb called the dragonleaf, which my dragons feed upon. When the woman who is to be my empress touches the leaves, the dragons will come to her, and there will be a sound that only I can hear. The phoenix bells, we call it. Thus, will I know her."

"You are looking in England now—as you did in Russland and in France." Her voice was neutral, her face half turned away so that he could not see her eyes, or her expression.

"Yes, the king and queen have graciously agreed to hold an elaborate ball, where I will meet with the young women and test them."

"And how are the women to know they should come to the ball?"

"Some weeks ago when I first arrived, Henrietta Maria drew up a list, and invitations were sent out. They would have reached their destinations by now."

"I see." Abruptly Blessing stood and, turning to him, smiled, although with difficulty. Her eyes looked moist, but in the failing light of the day he could not be sure. "I am afraid that it's growing late once more, and I must leave, Your Majesty. I am sure that my father is already waiting for me."

He nodded and rose, too. "Tomorrow afternoon, Blessing? Or will you be busy?"

Her smile faded. "My father has been talking about returning home. I—I don't know."

"I hope I see you," he said.

She nodded, then ran along the white path. He watched her, then looked around him. The golden light that had always been in the garden when Blessing was with him was gone, and now everything looked harsh.

The harshness of reality, he told himself, and slowly headed toward the palace, and realized with pain that she had not again called him by his name.

General Soong knew the emperor too well to not know that something had happened. He bid Ty-Sun sit down, then fetched plum wine for both of them. He knew that Ty-Sun had been going to the gardens each afternoon; in fact, he had been keeping an eye on him, even though the other man didn't know it. And Soong had seen the young girl, too.

"Tell me what's wrong, Ty-Sun. You know that you can tell me."

"I have no joy left."

Half of Ty-Sun's face lay in shadow, the other was outlined vividly in the candlelight, and Soong thought that he'd never seen him look so harsh or so lean. Ty-Sun had lost still more weight since coming to England, and long gone were any traces of the plump, indulgent ruler. Soong marveled at the strength of character that had waited for all these years to be revealed beneath the layers of fat. Who would have thought this hawk of a man had once been too sleepy to even do more than waggle a finger to send some poor servant off on a useless errand?

"I met a woman in the garden. She was the singer that I told you about. About a week ago I found her, and we talked. That's all."

"That's all?" Soong raised his white eyebrows. "Surely there's more to it than that. Your expression is one—" He stopped.

"I know my duty. I don't have to be reminded."

"I wasn't reminding—"

"I know that I'm here to seek a bride, and that's all."

"I know, too, but surely you can tell me—"

"She was of a good family, I suppose, although her father is a prominent Puritan. This afternoon we parted ways."

"I see." Prudently Soong kept quiet now, although he had many more questions he wanted to ask.

"That's all. Now, I must rest, for I believe Their Majesties have some festivities planned this evening, and it will be a very long night."

Soong nodded and watched as Ty-Sun left the room. There was a slump to his shoulder, a defeat in his eyes that had not been there that afternoon

And yet, he asked himself, Ty-Sun had no choice. There was only one woman who could be his bride—the woman who passed the test. In a week, all would be settled, Soong told himself. Or would it?

He tried to sleep because he knew he was tired, but nothing

would work. Instead, his mind raced, and his eyes stayed open. Even Ch'u seemed to mope, he thought, glancing at the dog twitching in his sleep.

Finally, he rose and went to the window and stared out. He was glad his rooms faced the river and not the gardens.

The moon rode high above the river, which flowed silver. Words, unbidden, came to his mind. *A thousand memories gather day and night,/A myriad sorrows brim dawn and dusk.*

All that evening he had thought of her, and in vain he had looked for her among the company at Court. But he knew she wouldn't be there. Not after this afternoon.

He glanced up at the stars, faintly shining tonight, and bowed his head in sorrow.

26

"What's wrong with you? You've been moping about for days. Are you ill?" Miles Dunncaster stared at his daughter, then tapped his foot impatiently. He expected an answer, and a prompt one, too.

Blessing raised her head from the prayer book she had opened on her lap more than an hour ago. Since then she hadn't read a single word. She sat on a hard bench by a window. It was cold there, but at least she could see outside.

"Nothing is wrong, Father."

"No?"

She shook her head. " 'Tis the weather; it's so dreary." She turned her head to stare out the rain-splattered window. Rain continued falling heavily, as it had for the past two days. Large puddles formed in the yard beyond, and pedestrians, their cloaks pulled tightly around them, hurried past. And only a short time before that she'd walked through the sunlit gardens with him, enjoying the crisp spring air and his company. Him. She shook herself. She mustn't think about him, or the ache she felt now. She glanced back at her father and attempted a reassuring smile.

Edmund, standing behind Miles, saw the tremulous smile and frowned slightly.

"Well, doubtless the sun will shine tomorrow and you'll feel better," Miles said. "I think you should spend the rest of the day in prayer. That should keep your mind from the weather."

"Yes, Father." She bowed her head until she knew he had left, then raised it and was surprised to find Edmund still standing there. "Ned, I thought you'd gone with Father."

"I wanted to speak with you. I know you're upset, even if that old bear can't see."

"Hush," she admonished gently. "He'll hear you—and we'll both get the rod then."

"I don't care, as long as you aren't hurt. You know that I could never bear that."

It was true, too, for she remembered the many times he had lied to their father so that she wouldn't be punished. She had never wanted him to take the blame, and afterward had gone to their father and confessed, and in the end he had still beaten her.

Edmund sat beside her on the bench. "Blessing, what's wrong? I know something's amiss. I can see it in your eyes and the way you carry yourself now. Can't you tell me? I'm your old Ned—you know that I would never say a word."

She hesitated. Throughout their lives, she and Ned had shared many secrets, being far closer in age than their two brothers. Ned never told their father anything she revealed to him in strictest confidence; she had done the same for him. There was no one else alive whom she could trust as much. Why did she hesitate then? Was it because this was vastly different? This was no matter of a childish transgression, but a matter of a woman's love for a man. What would her brother say to that? What would he say of the man she loved? Ned wasn't a strict Puritan, not like her father, but neither was he like her in that other sense. That strain only came through the women in the family. Her mother first, then her.

"I'm sorry, Ned, but I can't say anything right now. You know that I trust you above anyone else." He nodded. "But you must be patient with me. All right?" She looked at him and waited.

He smiled slightly. "Very well, I'll wait. You know I'll be ready whenever you want to talk to me." He stood and bent and kissed the top of her head. "No matter what it concerns."

"Thank you," she whispered.

She was already abed that night when she heard the soft knock at the front door. Curious as to who would be calling so late, she sat up and strained to hear what came next. Someone—her father, she presumed—slid back the bolt, then opened the door. She heard a man's voice, vaguely familiar.

Carefully she rose and walked across to the door of her room, which was on the second floor, close to the large room below which served as dining room and kitchen and parlor. She opened the door, held her breath to see if they had noticed, then slipped out onto the landing. Here she could look down without fear of being seen, for it was too dark to see anything on the landing, and she could hear as well what was said.

The visitor was Oliver Cromwell. Involuntarily her nose wrinkled, as if she smelled something sour. She might have known it would be him tonight. Cromwell came and went at their house at odd hours, all of it "business," or so her father claimed.

Wait, she told herself, they were talking about the royal ball. Holding her breath, she leaned forward slightly.

"—invitations," Cromwell was saying.

"My daughter received one, but I am happy to report that I burned it at once. I won't be having her go among those godless ones."

Blessing's heart seemed to hammer inside her chest. She had received an invitation after all?

"—we act," Cromwell said. "They'll all be at the palace that evening—it's the most logical time. My men will be ready. Will your sons?"

She didn't hear her father answer, so she assumed that he simply nodded. What did Oliver Cromwell want with her father and three brothers? What could these men possibly be up to? Hush, she told herself, she must listen some more.

"We'll wait until the women are presented, and then once the frivolities commence, we will strike, and with God's good grace, we will be victorious."

"My sons will have their swords, as will I. Will you be there?"

Cromwell was pacing by the fireplace now and the yellow light gave his face a jaundiced look. "No, Miles. As you might imagine, that might not be politically expedient for me. I'll be outside, though, in case something should go wrong. Remember to wear your masks. My men will be likewise concealed."

"And then once the deed is done, we'll ride at once to the coast, and then circle back in order to confuse any pursuers."

"Good, good."

Cromwell sat then by the fire, and her father and he began discussing other matters.

Stunned by what she had just overheard, Blessing rocked back slightly on her heels and stared with disbelief into the darkness. Her father and Cromwell planned to kill Ty-Sun on the night of the royal ball, less than a week away! Why? He had never done anything to them. But even as she asked, she knew the answer. Because he was different, because in some way he threatened them, and so they must dispose of him.

She must tell him. She couldn't wait until the evening of the ball; that would be too late, and what if she didn't reach him in time? No, she had to see him before then, and the sooner the better. As she rose, a floorboard beneath her foot creaked. She paused, breath held.

Cromwell's head came up, and he stared up at the dark landing. She willed herself to be invisible, knew that was silly, and yet the way his eyes searched the darkness . . . She shivered.

"Where is your family?"

"The boys are out, and the girl is fast asleep. Has been for hours."

"Good." Cromwell looked away and began talking about the king's latest outrageous action.

She breathed a sigh of relief, and carefully tested each board before she stepped on it. Finally, she closed the bedroom door quietly, then tiptoed across to her bed. Once back under the warm covers, she shivered, but not from the cold alone.

Outside, the wind moaned, splattering rain against the window, then stirred the branches of the huge tree that grew outside her room. The tips of the branches, like skeletal fingers, scraped against the glass, and try as she might, Blessing could not sleep for the rest of the night. All she could think of was what her father had planned for the man she loved.

Blessing wanted to rush off the very next day and warn Ty-Sun, but it wasn't possible. All day her father kept her by his side, and finally, when it was late, he told her to go to bed. She obeyed, went to her room, but she did not undress or go to bed. Instead, she stood by the door and listened to the sounds downstairs.

She heard him moving about, then settling down to read the Bible by the fireplace. After about an hour, he yawned, then rose. Finally, he started up the stairs. She ran back to the bed and pulled the covers over herself, in case he looked in. But he didn't.

She waited until she heard his door close, then sat up. It wouldn't take him long to fall asleep, and once asleep, he'd stay that way. Breath held, she rose. She took her shoes off and held them in one hand, then crossed to the wooden cupboard containing her few clothes. She took out her heavy dark blue cloak, and threw it around her shoulders.

Then she went carefully down the stairs. Luck held with her because none of the stair treads creaked. The front door was bolted, as usual, and that stopped her momentarily. What would she say to her father if he came down and found it unlocked. Yet, she had no choice. She would have to chance it, and if her father did awaken and come downstairs, she would simply say she had gone for a late night stroll. Not an impossibility, although her father would be skeptical.

Still.

Quickly, she unbolted the door and slipped through it, then pulled it shut behind her. Then she set her shoes down, pushed her feet into them, and began walking rapidly away from the house. She didn't have a long walk to the palace—she would be there in about fifteen or twenty minutes.

The city was fairly quiet now that darkness had fallen. She heard the faint rumbling of carts and wagons, and the occasional shrill call of a horse. Few people were out at this late hour, and for the first time she realized how dangerous this nighttime errand was. There were cut-purses and worse prowling the dark and dirty streets of London. And she had no weapon with her. She had never been afraid of the night, but that had been the night as she knew it at their country home, a night when thousands of stars could be seen overhead, when there were only the sounds of owls and the prowling cats and mice in the grasses.

She pulled her cloak more tightly around her, and began walking faster. She reached the palace without incident, and slipped in unnoticed at the fringes of a crowd of drunken courtiers. She darted away from them, then looked around. There were so many floors and rooms to search. . . . Where would she begin?

She remembered that once Ty-Sun had mentioned that his rooms overlooked the river. Ty-Sun. She shook herself, and after she had wandered for some time, she realized she was not going to find his suite on her own. Finally she asked a friendly looking maid where she might find the emperor's quarters. As she slowly climbed up to the second floor, she wondered if she should have come here. She could have sent a note to him instead. Yet, who could she have trusted with that? Edmund, perhaps; but no one else certainly.

But she had come, and now she must face him. Taking a deep breath, Blessing knocked on the door. It was opened almost at once by a short Oriental man dressed entirely in blue. She explained that she had to see the emperor at once, but the man didn't speak or understand English, and as the minutes passed and she tried to make him understand, her frustration grew. Suddenly she heard someone calling out in English.

"May I help you, mistress?"

Behind the servant stood the Jesuit priest Ty-Sun had often mentioned. Fray Villadiego, she believed, was his name.

"Father?"

"Yes?"

Obviously relieved, the servant left, and the priest stepped forward; he was looking at her with a slight smile on his face, and she thought he had a very sympathetic face.

"Father, I have a message for the emperor that must reach him at once."

"A message at this hour?"

"I could come no other time. I'm sorry because of the late hour, but could you please tell him that Blessing Dunncaster is here. I-I think he'll want to see me, after all."

The priest said nothing as he gazed at her for a long moment, then finally said: "I am afraid that the emperor is not here at present, Mistress . . . Dunncaster, was it? He is away with the king."

"Oh no. When will he return?"

"In a few days' time, I believe."

In a few days the ball would be held. She couldn't wait to get the message to him. What could she do now? She'd never considered this possibility. Why had she been so foolish?

"You are distressed, my child. May I relay your message to him when he returns?"

She hesitated, then decided she had nothing to lose by trusting him. "It's a very important one, Father," she cautioned.

"Of a personal nature?" he inquired politely, almost indifferently. It was as if he did not wish to tread too heavily in this matter. Certainly he did not seem to want her embarrassed and she appreciated that.

"No," she said, although her cheeks turned red anyway. "It's a matter of life and death."

"Come, child, let us speak in a more private area." He drew her outside the rooms and walked down the corridor to a window at one end of the hall. There were no doors nearby, no place where anyone could linger and eavesdrop. Here he turned and faced her. He smiled sadly at her. "There are eager ears in the emperor's entourage, and while most of his people are loyal, well . . ." He shrugged elegantly. She nodded, understanding. "Now, what is this matter that has brought you out in the middle of the night?"

She brushed back a strand of hair and took a deep breath. "It concerns his safety, Father. I fear that someone may take his life."

He raised a thin eyebrow. "A plot against the emperor? But, come child, how do you know of such intrigue?"

"My father is Miles Dunncaster, a prominent Puritan, and I overheard him and another Puritan speaking last night about a plot of theirs against the emperor. They hate Ty-Sun because they think he is influencing the king. Too, I believe they think he's in league with the Devil." She nodded her head emphatically at the priest's smile of disbelief. "It's what I've heard."

"And because they fear him they wish him dead?"

"Yes."

"When?" he asked softly.

"The night of the royal ball. You see why I couldn't delay until he returned. These men will allow the emperor to review the women so that he might select his b-bride," here her voice trembled a little, "and then they will strike. They'll be masked, so that they can't be recognized. Oh, please, Father, won't you do something!"

"Yes, my child, I will. As soon as—nay, the moment the emperor returns from the countryside, I will give him your message," the priest replied gravely. He patted her lightly on the back. "Now go home and sleep and do not worry. I will take care of everything." And Fray Villadiego smiled.

27

The night of the ball came all too quickly for Blessing. She had thought she might be able to sew a gown for herself, but it had been impossible in that short time. Too, her father would have wanted to know what she was doing, and how could she have explained even the simplest of gowns to him?

During the day she noticed restrained activity in the house as her father and two elder brothers came and went on unspecified errands. Errands, she little doubted, which were related to that night's task. She didn't know when they would leave to meet Cromwell's men, but she wanted to be ready right after they left.

As usual, she prepared the evening meal of stew, and among the men, only Edmund seemed to be his usual self, talking and laughing, which brought stern looks from the elder Dunncaster. Finally, when they'd eaten, Miles pushed back his chair and said gruffly that he had business elsewhere. The three stood, Ned glancing at her briefly, then gathered their cloaks and left.

"Aren't you leaving with them, Father?" she asked when he stayed behind.

"In a moment, daughter. First, I have something else to do. I want to insure that you won't be tempted to leave the house tonight."

"What?"

Before she could move, Dunncaster grabbed her arm roughly and hauled her up the stairs, then pushed her into her room. She went sprawling onto the floor, and she stared, bewildered, at him.

Anger reddened his face, and he kept his hands clenched at his sides. "You think I don't know you went out the other night, whoring like your mother before you? And by God tonight, I'll make sure it doesn't happen again, daughter. For your own good, I'm locking you in until I return."

She flung herself at him. "No, Father, please, don't do that! Please!" Miles remained unmoved as he glared down at her. "What if the house should catch fire? What would I do then?"

"Then you would burn up like your mother. The Devil take her—and you, you devilspawn!" He pushed her away, and she stumbled, falling to the floor. She listened, still unbelieving, as Dunncaster turned the key in the lock.

Tears filled Spring Rain's eyes. The emperor was dressing even now in his ceremonial robes, and in a few minutes they would leave to go downstairs to meet with the king and queen.

And then—and then she would lose him forever. She wept.

Soon, it would be over, and then they would be on their way home before long. Of that, he had little doubt. Soong sighed as he stroked his moustache and drank another glass of plum wine. It had saddened him to see his friend suffer so, and suffer Ty-Sun had these past days, although always in silence. Soong saw the pain in the other man's eyes, pain that he could not have what his heart truly desired.

And there was pain, too, in the eyes of Spring Rain. He had known she loved the emperor, but did not know how deep until now.

He rubbed a hand over his face. All this unhappiness. Was the cause worth it?

He glanced at the teakwood box containing the dragonleaf. To save the Willow Garden and the world . . . yes, it must be necessary.

He sighed again and pulled on his boots. It was time to go.

Blessing sat up slowly and rubbed her arm, bruised in her fall. What was she to do? She knew she couldn't unlock the door, not from the inside, and not without an extra key.

She felt tears stinging her eyes. Her father didn't love her, much less care for her. She knew that now—how long it had finally taken her to realize it! She brushed a tear away, then took a deep breath. How he must have hated it when she was born. A daughter to always remind him of what her mother had been. A witch, yes, but no whore. She knew that in her heart.

But she couldn't sit here, feeling sorry for herself, she thought. She had to do something. She wasn't going to stay here all night.

No door. No way to get out. Except—there was a window. She walked over and stared out at the tree's branches growing across to the windowsill. She had no other choice. She opened the narrow window and managed to squeeze through it, then she crawled out onto the branch. Hand over hand she went until she reached the tree trunk, then she dropped down onto another thicker branch, only a few feet below, and slowly she wound her way down the tree, until she was only a few feet above the ground. She jumped, landing softly, then looked around. Good. No one had seen her.

She heard a rustle in the bushes and stopped, scarcely able to breathe. A black and white head poked out, and meowed loudly. She smiled. The cat from the palace had followed her home.

She stooped and the cat trotted over to her to be petted. "Come with me, little one." The cat cocked its head as it listened. "I think I will need your help tonight."

She stood and with the cat at her side began walking in the direction of the palace.

Tonight was the night he had been dreading for so long. It had come finally and all too quickly. He had slept little since that last afternoon when he had seen Blessing—a lifetime ago, was it not?—and he marvelled at how often his thoughts turned to her. Inside he ached, and at times he felt like he was burning up with a fever. He caught the others staring oddly at him, then he would turn away.

He missed her. He wanted to be with her, to hold her in his arms and whisper to her. He wanted to make love to her under the starry sky.

He wanted too much. The gods no doubt thought him greedy, and he knew that he was. It was too much to expect to have a wife whom he could love. Let it be enough that she would save his Willow Garden.

Who sits alone by the bright window?/My shadow and I, only we two./But the lamp burns out; there is darkness./ Even my shadow forsakes me./Alas, alas!/I am forlorn.

But it was too late now, too late tonight, and thinking of what was to come, Ty-Sun closed his eyes and dropped his head into his hands and waited for Soong's knock on the door.

28

As he sat on the throne next to those of the English monarchs, Ty-Sun glanced around the large ballroom. Thousands of candles provided light, giving the room a golden glow. Fanciful mirrors lined one wall, reflecting the thousands of flames, glancing off the crystal chandeliers and the tiled floors. The light gleamed on the beautiful jeweled necklaces and earrings, pins and pendants that were worn by both men and women alike in the crowded ballroom.

As he turned his head, he caught a blur of red. That would be him, he supposed, among all of this gold and silver and copper that was the English Court this terrible night. Earlier, before he had left his rooms, he had taken a long time to dress, trying to postpone the inevitable, but eventually he had selected red robes, dragons and pheasants embroidered in white. Soong had raised an eyebrow, but only Ty-Sun knew the white symbolized his mourning for Blessing.

Off on one side of the room were the refreshments, table after table laden with the most delectable of meats and fish and sugared delicacies. Servants would be fetching goblets of wine for the emperor and king and queen tonight, but as for anything to eat, that would have to wait until all this was done. He had little appetite tonight, and marvelled that that would ever happen.

He sighed and listened to what Charles was saying, something about the evening. At Ty-Sun's side stood General Soong, holding the box. Behind him were several other members of the entourage, a pale-looking Spring Rain included.

Lord Elphinstone, resplendent in a green velvet jacket with slashed sleeves, and emerald and topaz striped breeches tied at the knee with lace, stood nearby, having volunteered his assistance for the evening. Martin Bleeker, in a new jacket and breeches of fine blue cloth provided generously by his master, stood behind him and gazed longingly at Spring Rain.

Ty-Sun's expression was not of a man about to find his wife, but that of a leader doing his duty, which he was. Tonight, he would not be joyful. Except in that finding his bride would be the salvation of his country. Only through that could he find happiness. He stared straight ahead, unseeing, completely unaware of the beautiful gowns of the women who waited to touch the dragonleaf, of the covetous looks directed toward him by many of them. He thought of nothing but his own misery, and wondered where *she* was this night.

Charles coughed gently until Ty-Sun glanced his way. "I thought, Your Majesty, that first we would begin with the presentation of the women. You understand, do you not, that there are many of them so that this will take some time?"

All night, he had calculated earlier in the afternoon as he thought about the ball. All night he would be forced to stare at these women who would be staring at him. Hours and hours of this. Could he endure it? "Of course, Your Majesty."

"Good, good." Charles smiled, then stood, one hand still touching the throne. Instantly the talking in the great room died down. "We shall ask first that the women here tonight who wish to touch the dragonleaf form one long line. Yes, yes, my servants will help you, and when each woman takes her turn here before the dais, General Soong,"—here the general inclined his head,—"will open the box he holds, and the emperor will hand a leaf to each young lady. Now, shall we begin the royal ball?"

He sat down to uproarious applause and he smiled, no doubt thinking how popular he was tonight. He glanced at his wife, who also smiled and blew him a kiss. He grinned boyishly.

"You must watch the proceedings with some modicum of interest," Soong whispered to Ty-Sun. "Even though your heart lies elsewhere."

"Very well." He knew that his friend was right, but he found it hard to concentrate. Each woman he glanced at had the face of Blessing, and that was like a stab in his heart.

Slowly a straggling line formed to one side of the ballroom. Royal guards kept the mere onlookers from mingling with those in the line, and as he scanned the blur of faces that seemed to stretch on forever, he shuddered. Each and every one of these women had come here tonight hoping they would become his empress. None of them knew him at all. None.

He stared at them, in their velvet and satin and taffeta gowns, in burgundy, russet, mauve, canary, magenta, saffron and emerald. All the colors of the rainbow were represented, and as he continued staring at the riot of color without any spark of interest, he caught a glimpse of grey.

He frowned at the intrusion of that neutral color, frowned because the simple gown had caught his attention. He tried to find the grey again. He looked left and right, then there it was again, and the face above it. . . .

Ty-Sun sat up, his hands gripping the padded arms of the throne.

It was her. Blessing.

She had come tonight.

Now she saw him looking at her, and she was smiling, although a little wanly. His eyes locked on to her slight figure as she genteelly pushed her way through the crowd, twisting and turning and slipping through the tiniest of spaces so that she could reach him.

When she was only a few feet away, she stopped, then blushed and her gaze dropped. He could not keep his eyes from her.

"Did you receive my message, Your Majesty?" she called as she tried to get closer.

"Message? What message?"

"My warning about the—"

But at that moment she was swallowed up by the crowd which had surged forward, then was slowly pushed back by the guards. Ty-Sun looked for her, but could not see her until a few minutes later when he glimpsed her grey gown toward the back of the crowd.

"What was that all about?" Charles asked, leaning toward Ty-Sun.

"I don't know," he replied slowly. He looked to Soong. "Do you know of some warning?"

"What? No. Never heard a thing about it," the general said, his tone grumpy. It was obvious he wanted this ordeal to begin without further delay.

Ty-Sun frowned. What message could she have sent? And why hadn't he received it? "My warning about the—" she had begun. The what? An object or a who. But he had no further time to think about that because the first woman was being presented to him.

"Lady Alicia Lawson of York," the Royal Steward announced mournfully. She was a painfully thin woman, scarcely more than a girl, with a pinched face, and a nervous tic in one eye. She wore a sumptuous gown of gold satin, and her brown hair was adorned with diamonds that caught the lights of the candles overhead.

"Your Grace," she said, executing an extremely graceful curtsy.

Ty-Sun saw no reason to correct her as he handed the red and gold dragonleaf to her.

Alicia Lawson clutched the leaf to her flat bosom and closed her eyes, as if she were undergoing an ecstatic or highly religious experience. Soong and Ty-Sun exchanged rueful glances.

Ty-Sun did not think this was the woman who would be his empress. Still, he must wait. And wait he did, for five minutes more. Nothing happened, and finally she opened her eyes, then sadly handed the leaf back to him. It was warm from her hands, and he dropped it back into the box and selected another cooler leaf. She curtsied, then moved away without looking back, and Ty-Sun felt a pang of sorrow for that lonely woman.

The second woman, from a farming district in east Kent and far from skinny, held the leaf, but again, nothing happened, as was the case with the third and fourth women, both attractive in blonde ways. A dozen women went by and still nothing.

When the twentieth woman approached the dais she gazed at Ty-Sun unflinchingly as she took the dragonleaf. Introduced as Margaret Campbell, she had fiery red hair, pale grey eyes, and wore red brocade. She had a bold look that Ty-Sun found somewhat more appealing than some of the vapid looks he'd received earlier. Suddenly she began moaning. He sat up straighter, then glanced at Soong. Was this the one?

"Och, I see, Your Majesty, I see, hundreds of dragons floating above a beautiful land filled with willows. Dragons of many hues. Large ones and small ones. Many dragons."

Charles looked eagerly to Ty-Sun. "Is this the one then?"

"No, Your Majesty." For a moment his hopes had been raised, but now he knew she was faking it. "The dragons will come to the true empress."

"Next," Charles said, a tired tone to his voice, and Margaret Campbell reluctantly surrendered the dragonleaf and rejoined her friends who congratulated her on almost having become an empress.

Hour after exceedingly boring hour dragged by, and as the ballroom grew warmer and the air more stale, tempers shortened. It was quite apparent that Charles had long ago grown weary of the entire proceedings and clearly wished he were elsewhere, perhaps even in bed, while Soong was fidgeting with impatience. Ty-Sun felt as if he were living a veritable nightmare.

Only Lord Elphinstone, who was still managing to smile after all these hours, and Henrietta Maria, who had retained her lively interest as well as her freshness, despite the heat, looked as if they were enjoying themselves.

Ty-Sun shifted, restrained a yawn, then glanced toward his entourage. Spring Rain was no longer there, nor was Martin Bleeker, and he wondered where they had gone. Perhaps she'd returned to their rooms, or perhaps she had gone out for fresh air with Martin. He was a good boy, rather likable in his blunt honest way, and he knew the boy was in love with Spring Rain. He accepted a glass of wine from a servant, and as he sipped it, he glanced down the line of women still left. Blessing stood only some fifteen women away from him.

Slowly the line inched forward. That evening he had been introduced to more Margarets and Alices, Helens and Catherines, one or two each of Phyllis, Susanna, Hope, Winifred, Sylvia, Penelope, Ophelia, and Deborah, and more than a handful of Joans, and nearly two dozen Elizabeths, Marys and Annes, respectively. The names—and faces—were blurring within his mind. Most of the women seemed fairly attractive in one way or another, and had he not already met Blessing, he would not have minded marrying one or two of them.

But he had met Blessing. And that made all the difference in the world.

Several more Annes trooped by, and a Rachel and an Imogen, still fully five more Marys, then finally, it was time for Blessing to step forward to the dais. The Steward, who was getting a bit hoarse, announced her. "Mistress Blessing Dunncaster."

King Charles sat up at that, having recognized the despised Dunncaster name. As if fearing to see nothing but Puritans, he glanced at Henrietta Maria, who shrugged casually. Obviously she wasn't worried about it. Others in the growing crowd suddenly turned their attention to the young girl. This was, after all, the first Puritan to have been introduced that evening.

Ty-Sun gazed longingly at her. She wore the simple grey gown he had always seen her wear, and a freshly starched white collar and plain apron. Her cheeks were pink, perhaps from the heat, or from the excitement of seeing him.

For the first time, he noticed that she was carrying a black and white cat. The cat he had seen with her in the garden, he realized, and smiled. She knelt, setting the cat down.

As Ty-Sun selected a fresh dragonleaf and handed it to her, his hand trembled. He knew that both Soong and the girl saw it, but he didn't care. She accepted the leaf with a murmured "thank you," then held it lightly, almost as if she were afraid she would damage it.

Slowly a whispering began in the crowded ballroom, rising, and then the rustle gave way to a roar. Ty-Sun stared, unbelieving, at the dragonleaf, while Soong gave a joyful shout.

As Blessing clasped the leaf, the fragile herb began glowing until it looked as if it had acquired its own life. The room grew hushed, and overhead could be heard the sound of wings. Ty-Sun grew aware of a high-pitched sound buzzing in his ears, that peculiar sound the dragons made. The phoenix bells.

"Look above!" someone shouted.

Heads throughout the room craned upward, while overhead a solitary dragon circled, its wings rising and falling gracefully.

Ty-Sun recognized Madame Shou and wondered where the other dragons were. Why hadn't they come with the old dragon?

"Dragon! That's a dragon!" someone in the rear cried, and the chant slowly went up. "Dragons, dragons, dragons . . ."

"Where did they come from?" a fat man in the front shouted, and crossed himself. None of the windows or doors were large enough to have allowed this winged beast to enter.

Ty-Sun rose, staring first at the old dragon, then at Blessing. She had been the one, after all. She had called the dragons forth.

The dragon roared, and the crystal chandeliers jangled with the noise. Steam in the form of small clouds puffed from her nostrils, and once more Madame Shou roared, the sound shaking the ballroom.

"Wait," Blessing cried out, raising a hand, and Ty-Sun stopped, puzzled. "Wait," she repeated again, and gradually the various sounds within the room quieted until all that could be heard was the rhythmic flapping of the dragon's wings. She gazed up at Ty-Sun, and it was almost as if she looked through him, rather than at him. Her face was intense in its concentration, her eyes dreamy. "Madame Shou has brought you a message, Ty-Sun. You must return home at once, for the Willow Garden faces a great danger. Go home now. Do not delay."

Slowly the dreaminess faded from her eyes, and as she gazed up at him, Ty-Sun saw the love there.

The dragon circled again, then slowly drifted downward toward where the girl stood. Men and women, frightened of the great beast, pushed away, until only Blessing stood by the dais. The dragon was nearly level with her head now, and as the large wings dipped and rose, her loose hair fanned about her. She held her arms up to Madame Shou, who dipped her wings in salute, and then sped upward toward the ceiling and circled faster and faster, all the while she was growing smaller. Finally, she was only a speck of gold against the white ceiling, and that, too, disappeared in a puff of steam.

Her warning momentarily forgotten in the midst of his happiness, a vast relief welled through Ty-Sun as he stepped off the dais. He had found his bride, after all, and it was the very woman he loved. He took her hands in his and smiled down at her.

29

As Ty-Sun turned around with Blessing's hand tucked in his to make the announcement that he'd found his empress at last, he heard shouting. He glanced back at the doors nearest the throne. Armed men swarmed through the doors, having overwhelmed the guards there, and as he whirled around, startled, and looked at the other entrances, he saw armed men there, too.

What trick was this now?

He fell back at once, holding Blessing tightly at his side, as General Soong stepped closer to him.

"The Puritans!" the girl gasped.

"What?" Soong demanded.

"My message to Ty-Sun. I warned him that this would happen tonight. They've come to kill him!"

At that moment a group of noblemen sprang forward to act as guard for the royal couple. The nobles were weaponless, because swords and daggers weren't permitted in the presence of the king. Tonight had been no exception. The few armed guards were engaged in fighting the Puritans, who seemed to keep pouring into the ballroom. Charles wore an expression of shock, as if he had never dreamed anything like this would happen to him.

Ty-Sun looked from door to door. There didn't seem to be any escape.

Suddenly Spring Rain was standing only a few feet away. She was nearly out of breath and limped slightly as she crossed to them and gave Soong's crossbow and sword to him, and handed Dragon's Tongue to Ty-Sun. Martin was there, too, with several swords bundled in his arms, which he quickly handed out to the noblemen guarding the king and queen. He had a slash, bleeding slightly, across his forehead, and one of his eyes was blackened. A frowning Elphinstone stepped closer.

"Martin and I left some time ago to take a walk outside, and when we were returning from the gardens, we saw these men gathering," Spring Rain explained, "and then I realized what it was they were planning. We returned to our rooms at once to get weapons, then tried to get into the ballroom. They attempted to stop us, as you can see, but I knew we must reach you."

Ty-Sun nodded his thanks, then touched the curve of her cheek. Her eyes filled with tears, but he didn't notice because he was already advancing toward the royal couple. Charles sat stiffly, darting sharp glances around him, fearful that he was about to be assassinated, while Henrietta Maria's face was drained of color.

Shouts and screams rose above the angry clash of steel, and as Ty-Sun's gaze swept around the room, he saw the masked men, Puritans Blessing had said, moving ever closer to the small conclave by the thrones. In a matter of minutes the intruders would reach them. Would he be able to protect Blessing, or any of the others? Those unarmed men and women who could, had fled, most of them having been let through unharmed by the Puritans. The doors, he saw now, were barricaded.

"These men do not wish to harm you, Your Majesty," Ty-Sun said. "They desire my death alone." His eyes glittered as he spoke, and Soong had never seen such a light in his lord before.

"I'll help you, Ty-Sun," Lord Elphinstone said as he bowed low. "Yes," he said in a slightly mocking tone, "I do know how to wield a weapon—and there is something else." His eyes locked with Ty-Sun's, and the emperor nodded in acknowledgment.

Martin grabbed a short sword and gave Elphinstone a trembling smile. Elphinstone affectionately ruffled the boy's hair.

Soong began nocking the whistling arrows, while Ty-Sun pulled Dragon's Tongue from its scabbard.

"Come," Spring Rain said, grabbing Blessing's hand and dragging her away from the others. She had sworn to aid the emperor and his chosen one however she might, and she knew she must act now. "It's too dangerous for you to stay. We must return to the imperial suite. Don't worry. He will be safe."

Unprotesting, Blessing allowed herself to be led away, but as she searched the forms of the masked men fighting nearby, she wondered which was her father, her brothers. Which one was Edmund? Then she recognized his thatch of unruly hair, no matter that he was masked, and she cried out to him. He turned in her direction, and suddenly an arrow, whistling in its flight, pierced his chest. Edmund collapsed onto the floor.

She gave a shrill cry and tried to rush toward him, but unrelentingly Spring Rain pulled her away from the fighting and through the doorway. Being unarmed women, they were allowed to pass unmolested. Blessing was weeping now, and Spring Rain tugged at her arm.

In the ballroom the fighting grew fiercer, with more and more guards falling, injured or dead, to the bloodstained floor.

"We can't hold them off much longer," Ty-Sun called to Soong, who nodded. "Get back to the rooms, then to the ships."

Again Soong nodded. He was using his sword now, hacking away at the men who charged him. Grimly they fought side by side, and some of the English noblemen, attempting to help, flung themselves at the attackers. A few were slain at once, while others were able to wrest the weapons away from the masked men and wield them at Ty-Sun's and Soong's side.

Ty-Sun glanced at Elphinstone some feet away, and the man seemed to be smiling with delight as he thrust his sword through a Puritan. He must be mad, the emperor thought, or have a long-standing grudge with the Puritans. He rather thought it was a mixture of both.

"Stop this!" Charles called, finally finding his voice, although it could scarcely be heard above the din of battle. "Stop this! You are guilty of treason!" No one listened.

Around them mirrors were smashed, and chandeliers rained crystal upon them. One man screamed as a sliver of crystal penetrated his eye.

Ty-Sun slashed at a stocky masked man trying to spear him with his sword. He reached forward, and grasping the mask in his hand, ripped it from the man's face. He recognized the man from Blessing's description. Miles Dunncaster glared at him.

Ty-Sun faltered, and Dunncaster chose that moment to press his advantage. He drove his sword toward the younger man, who leaped to one side, but only after the tip grazed his side. A burning sensation spread along his ribs, followed by a brief stab of pain, but he pushed the discomfort from his mind. Instead he thrust his sword at his opponent, laying open his arm to the bone. He did not want to kill Blessing's father nor any other member of her family, and yet they had come here expressly to murder him. How had he harmed them?

With a great cry he once more thrust Dragon's Tongue toward Dunncaster, and the older man shrieked as the weapon drove through him. He slumped down, and Ty-Sun slowly pulled his weapon out of the lifeless body. Bright droplets of blood dripped to the floor from the sword's dulled surface.

A tall man cried out and leaped forward, and Ty-Sun knew this must be one of the Puritan's sons. Was he doomed to kill the family of the woman he loved? Grimly he fought the masked man, but soon he fell back when his opponent was joined by another, equally tall. Elphinstone saw his predicament and leaped forward, slashing left and right. The first tall man fell, injured in his sword hand, while the second retreated.

A new opponent made himself apparent, but was hacked at by a young blond man, who then fell at Ty-Sun's feet. He murmured a short prayer for the fallen hero, then glanced at Elphinstone, who nodded. Ty-Sun lifted Dragon's Tongue high over his head, and cried out, "Spirits of wind and earth, fire and water and steel, come hear my plea tonight."

Balls of fire erupted in the four corners of the room, and suddenly began flinging themselves at the attackers. The masked men ducked, afraid of being hit by the fireballs, and tried to creep forward. The fireballs followed them, as though the flames were faithful dogs at the heels of their masters.

Elphinstone, alone, stood by the thrones and held up his arms. He chanted in a strange language that made Ty-Sun think of Blessing's songs. Lightning spurted away from the nobleman, and one Puritan standing closest screamed in a high terrified voice as the lightning struck his weapon, then collapsed, dead. The lightning skipped from man to man, knocking them over until they began to fling their weapons away.

"Now!" Ty-Sun called, and as he and Soong turned, he caught Elphinstone's eye and nodded his thanks. The man was still smiling, as if he were doing nothing more than holding a conversation on the merits of wine. Ty-Sun wondered if he would ever see him again. He hoped he would. Then he and Soong fled the ballroom. Ty-Sun was growing tired, as he knew the general was, but there was no time to rest because they were obliged to fight their way back to their quarters. And when they finally reached the second floor nearly an hour later, they found that the rooms were already breached by the Puritans, and that most of their entourage had been slaughtered. Only a handful remained.

More blood, more lives on my hands, Ty-Sun thought dully, as he looked around. "We must get to the boats at once." He looked at the bodies, but saw neither Spring Rain nor Blessing. Had they escaped? Or were the Puritans holding them captive?

Martin Bleeker suddenly charged into the room. "They're coming after you! Come this way. I know a shortcut."

He led them down the corridor a short distance to a great tapestry hanging on one wall. He lifted one end, and behind it Ty-Sun could see the door, like the one in his own chamber at home. Home. Would he ever see it again? He wondered. Soong pushed the door open, and Martin led them into the concealed passageway.

The way was dark, but Ty-Sun held Dragon's Tongue aloft and it glowed, allowing them to see. Water dripped down the walls, and unseen things scuttled away from the light. Finally, Soong pushed open another door, and they found themselves on the docks.

The sky was a salmon pink, tinged with gold, and Ty-Sun stared, surprised to find that the night had passed and that it was early morning.

They ran toward the two junks and saw that the crews were already preparing to set sail. Ty-Sun and the others leaped aboard just as the mooring ropes were untied, and the junks began drifting away from the docks. Even now the docks were filling with armed men, and Ty-Sun thought it had been close. As the junks headed toward the center of the great river, the huge sails were unfurled. Momentarily they luffed, then the wind shifted, and the great silk sheets billowed outward, thrusting the ships away from the city of London toward the Channel.

"Look." Soong pointed back toward the palace. Red and orange flames shot up from the building, painting the pale sky with a hellish cast.

The fireballs and Elphinstone's lightning, Ty-Sun thought sadly, and he wondered what had happened to Lord Elphinstone, to King Charles, to Queen Henrietta Maria, to the others who had fought so bravely.

He raised his exhausted arms with difficulty. Silvery grey clouds appeared, and rain poured down upon the great building, quenching the flames before the palace was further destroyed. Something could be salvaged of it, at least, he thought, then turned around, fighting the exhaustion that threatened to overwhelm him.

Soong was patting Martin proudly on the back. The boy appeared a little sick, and had several bleeding scratches, but otherwise he looked hail. Part of Soong's moustache had been singed and it was now several inches shorter than the rest, and he had a gash on his neck, but he too looked fit, otherwise. The other men who had fought were all injured in one way or another, but none seriously, Ty-Sun was relieved to see.

"Where's Blessing and Spring Rain?" he demanded, his voice rising with concern. He hadn't checked for them before they left the town. He should have. What if they weren't on board? What if the Puritans had captured them and held them now back in London?

"The women are both here, Your Majesty," Fray Villadiego said reassuringly at that moment as he came up on deck. Behind him were the two women, a black and white cat following. Ty-Sun wondered how the feline had survived all this. A brown form bolted up through the hatch, and with a grin Ty-Sun saw that even Ch'u had been rescued. An irritated rumble from below deck meant the bear was still with them, too.

Martin gave a joyous shout at the sight of the concubine, and Ty-Sun felt his exhaustion drain away as he greeted the women joyously, but to his surprise Blessing's face twisted with hate.

"You are a murderer. You killed my brother!" She sprang forward and would have struck Ty-Sun, except that the Jesuit restrained her. She was sobbing now, her face against the priest's shoulder.

But as relieved as he was to see her though puzzled by her reaction, Ty-Sun's attention had been drawn away from her. He was watching Spring Rain. Martin was at the concubine's side and talking animatedly to her, and yet she did not respond or even seem to hear. She was pale, almost as white as clouds.

"Thank you, Spring Rain, for saving Blessing's life," Ty-Sun said, "and for bringing our weapons to us. We could not have survived had you not acted so bravely—and selflessly."

"I told you that I would do all that I could for her, my lord," she said thickly, her words coming with obvious difficulty.

Suddenly she gave a small gurgle, and pitched forward onto the deck. Martin cried out, and too late Ty-Sun saw the dagger in her back which had been hidden by a fold of her robe. He called her name, but when he stopped and touched her cheek, she was already dead.

"She's not. . . ," Martin began, then hid his face in his hands and began crying, his shoulders shaking. He bent down and kissed Spring Rain on the lips. Soong placed a fatherly hand on his head.

"Go below and stay there," Ty-Sun said to Blessing, who stared in shock at the dead woman. Her earlier words forgotten, she nodded and without speaking further went below. His face was lined with exhaustion and grief as he stared at Spring Rain. She had saved him, and Blessing, and in doing so, she had been injured unto death. And she had never said a word.

When the ships reached the relative safety of the English Channel, Ty-Sun and Soong tenderly wrapped Spring Rain in one of Ty-Sun's ceremonial robes. Martin, red-eyed, watched dully as the two men committed her to the Celestial Sphere. Her body, weighted, quickly slid beneath the surface of the water. The priest murmured a prayer for her soul.

Ty-Sun stared at the spot where she had left this world, until someone tugged at his sleeve.

"Your Majesty. Look."

Behind them he saw the sails of the ships pursuing them. The Puritans, he realized wearily, would not let them escape so easily. They were determined to get to him and to kill him.

"We must return as quickly as possible to the Willow Garden." And he remembered Blessing's words as she held the glowing dragonleaf within her slender hands. Had that been only a few hours ago? He needed to sleep, but knew he couldn't, not yet.

For the first time since he had begun his journey, Ty-Sun truly grew aware of the incredible power of the evil force that challenged him, and he only hoped that he had not responded too late.

Soong paced the deck anxiously. The ships of the Puritans were gaining on them. There would be yet another battle to be fought.

With a heavy sigh,Ty-Sun, the One-True and August Emperor and Magician of the Land of Ten Thousand Willows, turned to his general to take up, once again, the great burden of his duties.